FIND EMILY

JJ TONER

DEDICATION

This one's for my offspring, Roisin, Brian and David.

Other Books by JJ Toner

Houdini's Handcuffs, the first DI Jordan thriller

The Black Orchestra, a WW2 spy thriller
The Wings of the Eagle, the second book in the Black Orchestra series
A Postcard from Hamburg, the third book in the Black Orchestra series

The Serpent's Egg, a WW2 Red Orchestra spy story

Zugzwang, a short story featuring Kommissar Saxon, set in Munich, 1933
Queen Sacrifice, a second pre-war short story featuring Kommissar Saxon.

ACKNOWLEDGEMENTS

Thanks to my long-suffering editor, Lucille Redmond, who went way beyond the call of duty to help get this book in good shape, to Rachel Lawston for the cover design, and Karen Perkins of LionheART Galleries for formatting the paperback. Sincere acknowledgements to Peter Tyrrell, Michael Cleminger, Patrick Touher, Gerard Mannix Flynn and Sean Hogan who lived the nightmare and wrote about it. And finally, to my wife for enduring my mood swings during the 12-months that it took to write this book.

About the Author

JJ Toner lives in Ireland. He writes shorts stories and thrillers. Connect with JJ through his web site http://www.jjtoner.com/

FIND EMILY

Chapter 1

Emily Carter cycled home from school on her pink bicycle, the satchel on her back heavy with her school books, black earphones covering her ears. She hummed along with Britney Spears playing on her Walkman. It was Friday December 17. The thought of Christmas made her fingers tingle. And on January 17 she'd have her twelfth birthday!

Christmas this year was going to be special. Her parents had promised her a new phone with a camera, and she knew her mother would buy her a book -- and there was always a surprise. The bicycle was last year's surprise, although she had guessed what it was because her daddy hadn't bothered to adjust the brakes on her old bike when they began to squeak and groan. She had a couple of special gifts for her parents this year, a filofax for her mother, a photo album for her daddy. She smiled at the thought of how surprised and happy they'd be.

She passed by a house with an enormous German Shepherd. His head reached up to Emily's chest. He barked at her most days from behind a closed gate, but today the gate was open, and the dog ran out, snarling and baring his teeth at her.

Emily put her brakes on and got off the bike. She propped the bike against a railing and held out a hand to the dog. "Good boy," she said, firmly. "Don't be nasty, be nice."

The dog looked confused for a moment. Then he stopped barking and lay down on the pavement. Emily walked over to him and he rolled onto his back. She scratched his tummy. "Good dog. Now go on home."

The dog got to his feet. Loping back toward his home, he met his owner emerging from the garden, a look of alarm on his face.

"I'm really sorry," said the dog owner. "Are you okay? He didn't attack you, did he? The gate should have been closed. I always keep it locked."

Smiling at him, Emily got back onto her bike and resumed her journey.

As she entered the lane that led to her road, a flurry of tiny snowflakes danced around her like butterflies. She made a silent wish that it would snow properly this year and she would have her first ever white Christmas. That would make it perfect!

The lane was creepy narrow, with high white walls on each side. To get through it, she filled her mind with images of wizards on flying broomsticks.

As she drew close to the end of the lane, a white van reversed into it, blocking her way. She put her brakes on. A tall man got out of the van and opened the doors at the back. Emily was still trying to work out what on earth he could be doing when he turned and looked straight at her.

The blank expression on his face told Emily that she was in danger. She tried to turn her bicycle in the narrow lane, but before she had it turned half-way the man walked right up to her, grabbed her by the upper arms and lifted her into the air. The bike fell with a clatter. She was still wearing her satchel, but he threw her over his shoulder as if she was no heavier than a towel. She kicked her legs. She tried to scream, but she seemed to have no breath. Her glasses fell off. She knew what was happening to her; she could see everything like a movie viewed from above, as if it was happening to someone else. All she could think of was the look of shocked disbelief that would appear on her friend Aimee's face when she told her. The whole thing was so strange she could barely believe it herself!

And the next moment the man put her down on the ground and plastered sticky tape around her head, through her hair at the back and across her mouth. Now she couldn't scream even if she wanted to. He tied her wrists together behind her back with more sticky tape, picked her up again, threw her inside the van and closed the door.

The van started. Emily tried to free her arms but it was impossible. She tried to sit up but the weight of her satchel held her down like a tortoise stuck on its shell. Thoughts whirled around in her head. Her phone was in her satchel. But she couldn't reach it. Her pink bicycle was lying abandoned in the lane.

Daddy will know I'm in trouble when he sees the bike. If someone doesn't steal it first. Aimee will ring soon. Maybe. She'll know there's something wrong if I don't pick up. No, she won't. No she won't. Aimee will leave a stupid message like she always does.

Chapter 2

Detective Inspector Ben Jordan was more than half-convinced that he had stumbled on a new form of free-form jazz. He was already half cut when his fellow-drinkers persuaded him to play, and after an hour and a half pounding on the piano and knocking back shorts at The Bleeding Horse pub, his fingers flew over the keyboard, coaxing the tune into areas never previously explored.

He'd been around the melody a dozen times when it suddenly lost its charm. He stopped playing mid-bar. No one seemed to notice. The place was black, rocking with the roar of a hundred conversations punctuated by raucous laughter.

He'd long since lost his audience. He wasn't surprised. With a wry grin and his foot on the loud pedal he played the first few notes of Roll out the Barrel. The noise level dropped. Someone cheered. Someone else began to sing. Ben slammed the lid of the piano shut and got to his feet, shakily.

"How about a break for a cigarette, Ben?"

The voice was that of Ben's closest friend, Packie, his soft Donegal accent no match for the cacophony of the pub.

In the garden out the back where the smokers congregated, it was bitterly cold and both men immediately began to sober up.

Packie lit two cigarettes and handed one to Ben. "What was that you were playing at the end there?"

"Free-form, abstract jazz."

"Well it was certainly different, I'll give you that," said Packie. "D'you want to talk about it?"

"What? Talk about what?"

Packie took a long pull on his cigarette. "Why you fell off the wagon less than four weeks after leaving rehab. Why you can't stay sober."

Ben gave him the eye. The last thing he needed was a second conscience. His own was doing a powerful job, guilt firmly lodged like a lump of coal just below his ribcage.

Packie was blunt as a copper's pencil, but there was no harm in him. His question wasn't so easy to answer, though. Ben had no firm idea what drove him to drink. All he'd got from four weeks of deep therapy in rehab was that it was probably the result of a traumatic childhood.

He replied, "The shrinks said I should blame my father for walking out when I was three."

Packie said, "I reckon you needed one more serious drinking session to prove to yourself that you have it under control."

That made perfect sense. "I couldn't have put it better meself."

"It's like when we surrendered our weapons. We kept a few back just to prove that we were in charge of our own destiny." The word came out as dastiny.

"The Provos kept some weapons back?"

"We did, surely. I thought everyone knew that."

Packie dropped Ben off at the front door of his new house in Sandymount. He was fiddling about trying to get the key in the lock when Kate opened the door.

"You're drunk!" she exploded. "Where have you been? What've you been doing? You're impossible. Obviously, your stay in rehab was a total waste of money. God, Ben, you're a mess. Have you seen yourself in a mirror?"

He swatted her words away with his hands, closed the door behind him and used it to prop himself up. "It's not what it looks like. I was just... I needed..." What had Packie said? What Packie said made perfect sense. He tried again. "You know the way the IRA kept some of their guns back after the ceasefire?"

"What are you talking about, Ben? You're a hopeless drunk. And we both know why. It's that job of yours. As long as you're with the Guards, you'll never be able to control your drinking."

Ben shook his head. "No, Kate. It's the Provos."

Without another word she turned and ran up the stairs. That was when Ben knew he was in real trouble.

Chapter 3

The van stopped. The man switched off the engine and opened the back doors again. He lifted Emily out and carried her into a house. It was cold, and she shivered. He lowered her onto her feet and she ran up the stairs. The man laughed and followed her. Emily stumbled from room to room looking for a way to escape, but all she found was rooms with no furniture and bare floorboards. Grinning, he cornered her in one of the rooms. As he approached his stomach wobbled from side to side. It was disgusting.

Then the man grabbed Emily's arm and slapped her across the face. She was stunned. It wasn't a hard slap but she hadn't been slapped, not even by her mother, since she was seven.

The man removed the tape from her wrists. Then he ripped the sticky tape from her face and hair at the back.

"Ow, that hurt," said Emily. Then, "Why are you doing this to me? What do you want?"

The man pulled Emily's satchel and coat off and laid them on the ground. He put a manacle around her left wrist and locked it with a padlock. The manacle was tight on her wrist. It was attached to a short chain. The chain was attached to an iron hoop set into the wall.

"What is the matter with you?" she said. "Don't you know who my mother is?" It occurred to her that maybe he knew exactly who her mother was. Maybe she had been captured because her mother was rich and famous.

Still the man said nothing. He had heavy boots, a crooked nose and a bald patch on the top of his head. His clothes smelled of tobacco smoke and sweat. His fingers looked like beef sausages stained brown from smoking.

He pulled a camera from his coat and took several pictures of her. It flashed each time. It caught her unawares the first time, almost blinding her, but she stuck out her tongue and ruined the last few pictures.

Her phone rang; 'Oops, I did it again' her Brittany Spears ring-tone echoed around the room. Trust Aimee to ring at the wrong time!

Without a word, the man put his hand inside the satchel and removed her phone. He didn't answer it. Instead, he dropped in on the floorboards and smashed it under his heel. Again and again, his big boot crashed down on it until there was nothing left but bits of metal and broken plastic. Emily nearly cried.

He collected up the pieces of the phone and left. As his heavy footsteps receded down the stairs she called after him in a half-whisper, "My daddy will kill you when he catches you." It was unlikely that he'd heard her, but she felt better that she'd said it. She knew it was the truth.

The front door slammed, rattling the windows. The van started up and drove away. After that there was silence. She looked out the window. She could see trees and patches of blue sky between the clouds. Straining her ears she just caught the clatter of a distant train.

She wondered if the man would have found her phone and smashed it if it hadn't rung just when it did. She decided he would have searched for it anyway. The thought that she might have been left with a working phone was more than she could bear.

Then Emily noticed the plastic potty. Apart from the iron hoop in the wall and the chain, it was the only other thing in the room. Maybe there had been a baby in the house at some time and the potty had been left behind. Then she realised it was meant for her to use. Her nose wrinkled in disgust. She was far too old for a potty. She would never use that thing. But she knew she would have to if the man left her chained for any length of time.

Chapter 4

Jordan and Packie were back in The Bleeding Horse drinking coffee when the call came.

"This is Superintendent Lassiter. Where the hell are you?" Lassiter, from the Dublin Metropolitan Region, was an old sparring partner from Jordan's time in the Organised Crime Unit.

"I'm on a half day," Jordan replied.

"All leave has been cancelled. How quickly can you get here?"

"Ten minutes," said Jordan.

"Make it five. Use your siren." Lassiter disconnected.

Jordan was intrigued. Something had put a serious dent in Lassiter's fender, serious enough that he was looking for help outside his own command. "I'm needed back at base." he said to Packie, draining his coffee.

Packie said, "What's the panic, Ben? Can't the Guards function for a single day without you?" He was unaware of the irony. Jordan's letter of resignation had been sitting on Deputy Commissioner Rory O'Malley's desk for four days.

Jordan made it to Harcourt Square in less than five minutes, abandoned his car in the compound, and ran inside. He took the lift to the DMR on the third floor. When the lift doors opened he found Superintendent Lassiter waiting for him.

"Jordan, good. Are you fit?"

"Fit as I'll ever be," said Jordan.

"We have a missing child." Instantly, Jordan's jaw stiffened. "I want you to take the lead."

Jordan couldn't believe his ears. Since the St Patrick's Day murders, he had been sidelined to the Organisation Development Unit, the backwater to end all backwaters. Now he was being assigned to lead an active investigation? His surprise must have shown on his face, as Lassiter offered an explanation: "One of the Deputy Commissioners put your name forward."

That had to be Rory O'Malley. He was the only high-ranking Garda officer who knew what really happened in the St Patrick's Day case.

"When was the child taken?"

"Three o'clock." Jordan checked his watch. It was 4 pm. The pitch of Lassiter's voice moved up a semitone. "This is likely to be the biggest missing person search the country has ever seen. We needed an hour to get geared up. Talk to Ulick O'Shea." And Lassiter walked away.

Let me have men about me that are fat, thought Jordan. Yon Lassiter has a lean and hungry look.

O'Shea pointed to a seat in front of his desk. "How much do you know?"

Jordan said, "Assume I know nothing."

A bulky individual in his late forties, DI Ulick O'Shea was a good copper with a number of notable collars to his name, but Jordan had never been able to take him seriously. Commonly known as 'Ulick the Ape', black and wiry clumps of hair lay like caterpillars on the backs of his fingers, and he had eyebrows to match. It was known from sightings in the showers that he was covered in the stuff, back and front, head to toe.

"The missing girl is Stella Carter's daughter, Emily."

Jordan made the connection right away. Stella Carter: the young, high-profile and much-admired CEO of 'The Sweat Box' chain of fitness centres and with interests in pubs, hotels and overseas properties.

O'Shea handed Jordan a photograph of Emily Carter dressed in her school uniform, wearing a disarming smile and wire-rimmed glasses. The family resemblance was uncanny. She wore a brace on her teeth, but she had her mother's sultry, brown eyes.

"How old is she?" said Jordan.

"She's eleven."

"Sweet Jesus! Do we have any leads?"

"Not so far," said O'Shea. "We have a couple of men at the school, and another team combing the area, doing house-to-house. Emily was taken on her way home from school in a narrow laneway that connects Acacia Avenue with the Enniskerry Road, in Stepaside, where the family lives. The end of the lane is less than 200 yards from her front gate -- and within an ass's roar of the garda station, I might add."

Jordan said, "The father's not Irish. Am I right?"

"Shane Quigley. He's an American."

"You're sure she was abducted?"

"There can't be much doubt about it," said O'Shea. "Her bicycle was found in the laneway -- and her glasses. No sign of her schoolbag."

"Has there been a ransom demand?"

"No, not yet. There's a man at the house monitoring the phone."

"The family has no security?" said Jordan.

"Nope."

Chapter 5

The buzz of voices in the Incident Room died as Jordan and O'Shea walked in. Superintendent Lassiter was there ahead of them.

Lassiter addressed the team. "You all know Detective Inspector Ben Jordan, ex-OCU, now with the ODU." This produced a few smiles and some chuckles. "DI Jordan has been drafted in to head up this investigation. As Officer-In-Charge you will all report to him. He will report to me. Are there any questions?"

For 'drafted' read 'parachuted'.

One garda raised a hand and asked, "Has Detective Inspector O'Shea been removed from the case, sir?"

Lassiter replied, "As I've said, DI Jordan is in charge. Senior management has expressed the view that Ben Jordan's extensive experience with the Organised Crime Unit will be of benefit to the investigation." Not a view shared by Lassiter, obviously. "DI O'Shea will no longer be directly involved, but may be called on if and when."

If and when I fail, thought Jordan.

"Over to you, Ben," said Lassiter and he and O'Shea left the room.

Jordan ran his eyes over the team. There were seven guards and a sergeant called Dan Payne, all known to him, every one of them giving him the beady eye treatment.

Jordan took a deep breath and said, "I can see from the amused look on your faces you all think this is a big joke, some kind of game of office politics. Well, it's not. You know why we're here. We have to find and rescue an eleven-year-old schoolgirl. Nothing could be more serious. And we are up against the clock. I don't need to remind you that time is critical in kidnap cases. If we don't find Emily in the first 24 hours, chances are we won't find her alive. Emily's relying on us. She has no one else fighting her corner." He paused to let his words sink in. "I promise you we will find her, but only if each one of us does his or her job speedily and efficiently." He addressed his next remarks to the sergeant. "As the senior man here, Dan, I'd like you to co-ordinate and collate the book of evidence."

Payne nodded curtly. Jordan wrote his mobile phone number on the whiteboard, and the sergeant did the same.

Jordan spoke to Payne. "I'll see if I can arrange a TV appeal for the nine o'clock news. After that, we will need a team to man the phones."

"How many lines?" said Payne.

"Six, at least. Who've we got on the phone at the house?"

"David Irwin. He has the technical know-how and he's trained as a hostage negotiator."

"Good." Jordan had heard favourable reports about Garda Irwin. "I'll need the address."

Payne wrote it down and handed it to Jordan.

"The super said a nationwide search was in progress."

"It is," said Payne. "Every division in every region is involved. But..."

"But what?"

Payne shrugged. "You know yourself, Ben, it's a hopeless task. Most of the teams are concentrating on stopping and searching vehicles. The rest are searching houses, farms and so on. But there's over a million and a half households in the country, half a million in the Dublin area alone, and the total manpower we have out there amounts to about 5,000 men."

"Right, I'm heading out to Stepaside," said Jordan. "Keep me posted the minute you have anything."

Chapter 6

Stella Carter took a double dose of codeine and retired to her room. She was suffering from a headache that hit her from the moment she realised that Emily had been taken -- a blinding, pulsing headache that interfered with her mental processes. Her usual ordered and decisive mind vacillated between action and inaction, running through the gamut of emotions from crippling fear to anger and back again to utter despair.

For the umpteenth time she tried Emily's phone and left a tearful message on her voicemail. "Emily, darling, we're searching for you. Ring as soon as you can."

She turned out the light, lay down on her bed and closed her eyes. The codeine began to kick in.

She awoke with a start and was immediately swamped with a new emotion. Guilt. It had been no more than a few minutes, but how could she sleep while Emily was in danger? The front doorbell had woken her. Emily! No, Emily wouldn't ring the doorbell, but maybe someone with news. She swung her legs off the bed, tidied her face and hair, and hurried down the stairs. Garda Irwin sat by the house phone. Stella had been aware of the garda's good looks, his bulk, but to her now he was not so much a man as a man in uniform, a comforting presence. He represented the considerable Garda effort that was searching for her daughter, the tip of a giant Garda iceberg.

There was a new officer in the room, a tall man with a shock of dark hair. He introduced himself as Detective Inspector Ben Jordan and said, "I am officer-in-charge of the investigation, Ms Carter."

"Do you have any news?"

"Nothing yet. Our officers are combing the country. Be assured, we will find Emily."

"You think so? You really think you'll find her?"

"I'm certain of it."

Stella went into the kitchen. Inspector Jordan followed her.

While she put a kettle on to boil, Jordan said, "Is Mr Quigley here? Could I speak with him?"

Stella shook her head. "I don't know where he is." As usual, when she most needed him, Shane wasn't there. He was out somewhere playing cops and robbers like some overgrown boy scout. He was so full of himself. Just this once, why couldn't he play the role of father of the missing girl and be there to comfort Stella?

Jordan said, "Tell me about Emily."

"What d'you need to know?"

"Her interests, her friends. What's she like?"

"Emily is a bright, happy, clever girl. She loves to read. She has lots of friends at school. She's good at languages and sports. Next year she'll be starting secondary school…" Stella stumbled to a halt.

"Go on. What else does she like?" the inspector said, quietly.

"She's learning to play the piano, and she's good with animals. She'd love a pony, and she's crazy about dogs. She's the apple of her daddy's eye, and she adores him, of course."

"How would she respond in a crisis?"

"I don't know. I know she has a strong will. She's not someone to take orders or do anything she… anything she…"

"Take your time," said Jordan.

"Even as a toddler it was impossible to make her do anything she didn't want to." Stella clenched her teeth. "She has a stubborn streak from her father and an independent mind that I suppose she got from me."

"Tell me about your businesses," Jordan said, handing Stella a mug of tea. "Any major financial concerns, any vengeful business rivals?"

"Money's always tight," said Stella, "but we manage, and as for vengeful rivals, I don't know what you mean."

"Is there anyone that might feel cheated or resentful or jealous of your success?"

Stella shook her head again. "No, I can't think of anyone. You think someone like that might have taken Emily?"

"What about disgruntled employees? Anyone you've had to fire?"

She gave this some thought. "Hiring and firing comes with the territory, Inspector. I could name three in the last ten years."

"Perhaps you could let me have their names," said Jordan.

Jordan asked Stella to consider making an appeal for information on the television. Her immediate reaction was shocked rejection, but when the inspector explained the advantages of such an appeal and the successful outcomes they'd had in the past, she agreed to go ahead with it and retired to her room to write a short script.

#

Jordan rang the office of the Garda Commissioner. The Commissioner's staffer promised to contact RTE, the national TV broadcaster, to make the necessary arrangements. She also agreed to ask the Commissioner if he would participate in the appeal himself.

Jordan reached for the phone in his pocket to give Sergeant Payne the names of the three disgruntled ex-employees. The phone went off in his hand.

It was the sergeant, and he had news. Several of the neighbours in Stepaside had spotted an unfamiliar, unmarked white van in the village in the past week to10 days. The van had been seen cruising around the area and parked in unusual places for extended periods.

"Are we clear what size of van we're talking about?" said Jordan.

"The smallest kind. The size of a car, like those postal vans."

"Okay, talk to the Domestic Violence and Sexual Abuse Unit," said Jordan. "I should be back there in about twenty minutes. Tell them to put together a list of likely suspects."

Chapter 7

Detective Inspector Liam Flood of the Domestic Violence and Sexual Abuse Investigation Unit was expecting Jordan when he walked into his office on the fourth floor.

Flood pointed to a seat in front of his desk. "I got your message, Inspector."

"Call me Ben." Jordan liked the look of Flood right away. He was fair-skinned with thick sandy hair and a smattering of freckles that ran across the bridge of his nose. He was incredibly young for an inspector, an impression accentuated by the freckles, but his serious expression and lined brow showed maturity, and there was sharpness in his eye.

All graduates emerging from the Garda Training College could be relied on to recite the Training Manual cover to cover, and they knew how to snap their heels and say 'sir' every few seconds, but few were well-equipped for life in the real world. Flood looked as though he might be.

Flood handed Jordan a manila folder. Jordan flipped it open and ran his eyes over the names. He knew none of them.

"Have you met the parents?" Flood asked.

"I met Stella Carter, but Emily's father wasn't there. What do we know about him?"

"That's Shane Quigley. He's an American citizen, an ex-NFL star." The reply came from a young female garda as she walked into the office carrying a mug of coffee.

Flood said, "This is Garda Mary Walescu."

Jordan took the coffee from Walescu. Another handsome, fresh face wearing a frown. Her hair, black as jet, was tied in a bun and she had big, dark eyes to match. She was in her late twenties, about ten years older than Jordan's daughter, Lucy.

"You're not Irish?" said Jordan. He tried the coffee, but it was too hot to drink.

"I'm from Romania," said Walescu.

Flood was saying, "Emily was issued with a US passport in the past couple of months. We'll need sight of that passport."

Jordan raised an eyebrow and Walescu explained. "The majority of child abductions in Ireland are by parents, and where one of the parents is a non-national, the children are often taken away overseas."

Flood added, "Admittedly that's a long shot in this case, but we'll need to check it out."

Jordan said, "How come Emily isn't called Emily Quigley?"

Garda Walescu laughed. "If you knew Stella Carter you wouldn't ask that question."

"You've met her?"

"No, no. But she is in all the women's magazines. She tells how to set up a business, how to raise children, how married women should keep their own family names. She is a tough lady."

"Tell me about these sex offenders," said Jordan to Flood.

"There's a thriving underage sex industry operating in the city. We know of seven kids that have disappeared in the past year."

Jordan put his coffee down on Flood's desk. "Why haven't I heard of these cases?"

"We've deliberately kept the investigation under wraps. Whatever chance we have of catching these scum we'd have none if the press got hold of the story. The kid's are all foreign, imported illegally and kept under the radar. They're held in captivity for a while before being sold on and shipped overseas."

"So how's the investigation going?"

"We're getting there -- slowly," said Flood. "We've been working on very little else for four months now."

Walescu said, "Five months. The whole thing is a massive tangle involving dozens of countries." Walescu waved her arms about. "We work with the Interpol and Europol. We try our best to identify the children, but many of them are never registered as missing in their home countries."

"So how do you know about them?" said Jordan.

"We see the pornography," Walescu replied, a grim expression on her face.

There was something odd about Garda Walescu. There was a hint of her origins in her accent, but there was something else that was not quite right. Jordan couldn't work out what it was. He glanced at her again. A lively look, an expression of concern, her hands clasped in front of her, she looked like a young nun.

Chapter 8

The first two names on Flood's list of suspects lived in the Tallaght area, a working-class suburb to the west of the city. Jordan turned on the Dispatch radio as Flood struggled through commuter traffic confounded by a light sprinkling of snow. The radio gave out nothing but the occasional short locator message -- a sure sign there was a big op on.

Jordan looked at the list of suspects again. "Only five names?"

"There are lots of others," said Flood. "Those are the most likely. All five have vans. The rest are banged up doing time or too old to worry about."

As they entered Tallaght Jordan felt his spirits rise and a growing tingle in his fingertips. It was eight months since he'd been involved in any real police work. Before his spell in rehab he'd completed a study on the possible coordination of CCTV coverage in built-up areas; the last four weeks had been spent struggling to make sense of a stultifying report on the proposed rationalization of public records. That was all behind him now that Someone-In-Authority had finally decided to give him some real police work to do.

Miley Richardson's van had been red when it left the factory 18 years earlier. Now it was mostly rust-coloured. Missing all four wheels, it crouched derelict on Richardson's front lawn like a grotesque sculpture doing its best to blend in with the weeds. Jordan reckoned the vehicle hadn't moved in at least five years.

The house was a bog-standard three-bed semi built in the seventies, the paint that the builder had given it peeling and flaking from the walls and window frames.

Richardson opened the door dressed in a filthy vest and baggy pants, a cigarette quivering on his lower lip. When he saw who was standing on his doorstep, he looked up and down the street. "For fuck sake," he said, "I'm trying to keep a low profile here."

"It's an unmarked car," Flood said, stepping inside, forcing Richardson backwards. "If anyone asks, tell them we were here to sell you double-glazing."

"Like anyone's gonna believe that!"

Richardson was a slight man, five feet seven in his bare feet. He'd been convicted of low-level indecency. It was his first offence, but he'd received a three-year sentence because minors were involved. He'd been released recently after serving just nine months.

Flood said, "Where can we talk?"

Richardson led them into his living room where a cocktail of toxic odours assailed them. The only furniture in the room was a mangy settee, its filthy, collapsed cushions a breeding ground for a million micro-organisms.

"What d'you want?" said Richardson, lowering himself onto the settee.

Flood said, "When were you released?"

"Couple of months ago."

Jordan took a look around the room. Almost everything that wasn't nailed down had been sold off. Discarded cider cans littered the bare floorboards. An ancient portable TV flickered soundlessly in one corner.

"Where were you between two and four today?" said Flood.

"Here."

"Was anybody here with you?" Jordan said.

Richardson laughed. "Yeah, sure, me and my mates were having a party."

"What about between twelve and two?"

Richardson gave this some thought, sucking on his damp cigarette. Then he said, "I was here."

"On your own?"

"Yes."

"And in the morning?"

"Same answer."

"So you've been here, alone, all day," said Flood.

"Pretty much." Richardson's eyes flicked from Flood to Jordan and back again.

"A comedian," said Flood to Jordan.

"You're telling us you've no alibi for any time today," said Jordan.

"Don't need one." Richardson pinched the head off his cigarette and slipped the half-butt behind his ear. "I haven't done anything."

Jordan jerked his head at Flood and they both stepped toward the door.

Jordan said, "We're wasting time here. Let's go."

"He has no alibi," said Flood.

"Yes, but look at him. This guy couldn't abduct an egg from a battery hen." Jordan opened the door.

"You're not taking me in?" Richardson struggled to his feet, clutching his can. "What's this about, anyway?"

"Not this time," Jordan said, "but don't go anywhere. We may need to talk to you again."

Richardson looked disappointed. Considering his living conditions, the prospect of spending a few hours in the pokey would have been like an invitation to a five-star hotel.

Chapter 9

Flood started the engine. The second name on the list was Peter Green, 56, a shopkeeper, convicted of abusing his own daughters, had been sentenced to four years. They had let him out on parole after serving less than half of that. Jordan remembered the public uproar that greeted the leniency of the sentence, and how, to protect his daughters from the press, Green's name had never been released.

As they approached the shop, Flood said, "I've had my eye on this guy for a year or more."

"Why?"

"He travels abroad a lot, and mostly to Eastern Europe. I'm sure he's involved in people trafficking. I just haven't been able to prove it yet. He's a slippery customer." He pointed out a white Ford Transit parked across the street. "That's his van." The licence plate was 04 D, this year's model.

"Nice wheels for a small shopkeeper," said Jordan. "But it's not the van we're looking for. It's too big."

They found Green behind the counter in his shop, a corner newsagent's with newspapers, magazines, sweets and cigarettes neatly arrayed, and a glass case of Danish pastries and sausage rolls. As they entered Jordan flipped the 'open' sign to 'closed' and locked the door. Green made no objection.

A flabby man, carrying 50 excess pounds, balding, and with grey prison pallor, Green wore the weary look of a man well used to visits from the Guards.

"Do you know this girl?" Flood showed him Emily's photo and he took it in his podgy fingers.

Green squinted at the picture as if he had poor eyesight. "No, I don't think so."

"Where were you today at three?" said Jordan.

"I was here all day." Green's eyes never left the photo. Jordan watched him closely. His face showed conflicting emotions. There was anxiety, certainly, but Jordan sensed arrogance, and there was something else, something visceral and unspeakable. He snatched the picture back and Flood tucked it into his folder.

"Can anyone corroborate that?" said Jordan.

Green shrugged. "Customers."

"Names?" said Flood.

"I don't have their names."

Flood said, "So you've no alibi."

"What am I supposed to have done?"

"Let's go back to the station and discuss it," said Jordan.

They put a protesting Green in the car and drove back to base at The Square.

Green sat upright at the table in Interview Room 1, his fingers occupied with a pack of cigarettes, the overhead fluorescent lights casting a blue sheen on his bald head and deepening his grey pallor.

Flood sat facing Green and opened a bulging folder. He read through several pages, starting from the top, Green's most recent history. Jordan remained silent, propping up the wall directly behind Green, watching the clock on the wall above the two-way mirror. The only sounds in the room were Green's breathing, which was laboured, and the gentle fizzle of the fluorescent lights. Flood continued to work his way through the folder, turning and reading each page slowly.

Green broke the silence, the tremor in his voice betraying his nervousness. "Why have you brought me here? What am I accused of? You can't hold me. I have rights."

The second hand on the clock completed another circuit of the dial. Flood turned another page.

Green took a cigarette from the pack and a box of matches from a pocket, but Jordan put an arm over Green's shoulder and removed the matches before he could use them.

"This is a no smoking area," he said.

Flood closed the folder with a thump and Green leapt in his seat. Flood fixed Green with his gaze and said, "What a nasty little man you are, Green. I would have given you life for what you did to your daughters."

"I served my time," said Green, crossing his arms high on his chest.

Flood continued, "And they let you out after twenty months. Now, that was clearly a mistake. You just can't keep your hands off little girls, can you?"

"I want a lawyer," said Green. "You can't question me without a lawyer."

Flood glowered at him. "Did you see me put a tape in the machine or switch on the camera? Did I check you in at the desk? Did I caution you? Did I?" Green shook his head and Flood continued, "This is not a formal interview. You are here to help us with our enquiries."

"So I can leave if I want to…" Green rose from his seat.

Jordan placed a hand on his shoulder and Green sank back into the chair.

"This is harassment, police brutality. You can't keep me here."

Flood said, "We won't detain you long. You can leave when you've answered our questions."

"It's not safe to leave the shop for any length of time. And I'll lose all my customers." Several loose folds of flesh came together into an approximation of a frown on Green's face.

"An hour or two won't make any difference," said Flood.

"If I lose my business I'll blame you. I'll complain to the Garda Ombudsman."

Flood placed Emily's photo on the table facing Green. "Tell us where to find the girl and we can have you back behind the counter in thirty minutes."

Green raised his voice. "I know nothing about the girl." His lungs bubbled audibly.

"Look at it," said Flood. "Look at the picture."

Green glanced at it. "Like I said, I don't know the girl."

"Her name's Emily," said Jordan.

"I've never seen her before."

"You like young girls, we know that," said Flood in a conversational tone. "Emily went missing at about three o'clock today and you have no alibi. What are we supposed to think?"

"There must be others…"

Flood's demeanour hardened instantly. "Others? Other vermin like you, you mean?" He slapped his open palm on the table top. Green jumped. "There's any number of nonces out there, but there can't be another like you anywhere in Ireland. Your level of depravity is unusual."

"Very rare," said Jordan, quietly. He watched the second hand on the clock complete another cycle. It was exactly 6 pm, three hours since the abduction.

"What d'you think, Inspector, where would you go to find another pervert who'd do what Peter here did to his daughters, his own flesh and blood?"

Green lifted his chin, stretching his dewlaps. "You can't--"

"It's a compulsion," Jordan murmured over Green's shoulder.

Green turned his head to look at Jordan, but Flood slammed a closed fist on the table. "Eyes front! Look at me." Then, speaking quietly to Jordan, "I hear it's impossible to reform this type of compulsion. Nothing can be done to rehabilitate these monsters. All we can do is keep them locked up and out of harm's way."

"I know nothing about this child," Green said, grinding his teeth. "I've done nothing."

"Tell me, Peter," Flood said, continuing in conversational mode, "Do you have a computer?"

"Ye-es, for the business..."

"I expect you use it to contact your friends. That's normal. What could be more normal than keeping in contact with your friends on the Internet? I bet you have friends all over the world." Green shot Flood a look of alarm. Flood's voice hardened again. "I bet you exchange photos with your friends all over the world. Am I right?"

"No--"

"There are worldwide groups that are into this sort of thing. They share disgusting pictures, pictures of children. Now what are they called?"

"I'm not like that. I don't..." Green mumbled.

"Paedophile rings," Jordan said.

"That's it!" said Flood. "I expect you share photos of your daughters with your paedophile friends on the Internet. Am I right, Peter?"

"You can't do this..." Green wheezed. "I'm not answering any more questions."

Flood leaned across the table toward Green. "You haven't answered any of our questions yet. Maybe you'd prefer to make it official. We could get you a lawyer, put you under caution and impound your computer?" Green shook his head. "When we look on your computer, what will we find? How many filthy, perverted pictures of children will we find?"

Jordan noticed the change of tense. Green did too. He rose from his chair again and again Jordan pushed him back into his seat. "I'm not like that," he said. "You have the wrong man. I need the computer to run the business."

"So tell us what you know about this girl, and you can go back to your shop," said Flood.

"I can't tell you what I don't know. Why won't you believe me?"

"I believe you," said Jordan. "But you must have some idea who took this girl. Just tell us who we should be talking to."

"I don't know. I've told you, I know nothing," Green shouted through bubbling lungs.

Flood leaned across the table and balled a fist in his face. "Give us a name."

Green lowered his eyes. "I'm saying nothing more without my lawyer."

Flood smashed an open palm on the table. "Look at me!" he roared.

Green flinched, but he continued to stare at the table-top.

Chapter 10

They left Green in the interview room, with a uniformed garda, and returned to Flood's office.

"Let him stew for a while," Jordan said.

"Let him rot," said Flood. "If I had my way I'd have people like him castrated."

In other company and under normal circumstances the open expression of such an extreme view would have warranted disciplinary action, but a lot had changed in the past three hours; the normal rules of behaviour no longer applied. Jordan wondered if there was something personal going on between Flood and Green. "I take it you and Green have history," he said.

"As I said, I've had my eye on him, but I've never interviewed him before. I was planning to wait until I had something concrete to throw at him."

"I think you need to go easy on him, Liam. He doesn't look well."

"Let he who is without sin cast the first stone. Well, I'm up for that. He's a sinner and a fat bastard sinner, at that." Flood spat these last words out.

"Overweight, certainly. Obese, even," said Jordan, "but I'd be more worried about the state of his lungs."

Garda Walescu opened the door without knocking and came in "The father of Emily is here," she said. "He's with Deputy Commissioner O'Malley."

"Didn't he used to be an American football star?" said Jordan.

"Yes. A tight end, I believe," said Flood.

"I'll say!" said Walescu. She glanced at Flood and he grinned. Jordan wondered about their relationship, whether it might be more than professional.

Jordan said to Flood, "D'you want to take this?"

Flood replied, "No thanks, Ben. Not my bag -- public relations. And it's your investigation. I'm only assisting."

#

Shane Quigley, Emily's father, stood with his back to the window in Deputy Commissioner O'Malley's office.

Following terse introductions, Jordan said, "We began a trawl of the register of offenders today. We have taken one man in for questioning."

Quigley stepped forward, "You've interrogated this suspect? What did he say?" The voice was deep, like warm honey, the accent unmistakeably American.

Jordan said, "This man is assisting with our enquiries. We have no reason to suspect that he is directly involved."

"But he is under arrest, you've read him his Miranda warning, right?" Quigley was an imposing figure, tall and broad. With his back to the window, his face was in shadow, but the tension in his posture and voice were clear.

"No, sir. As I said, we have no grounds to arrest him."

The Deputy Commissioner said, "Mr Quigley has worked with the NYPD. He has very generously offered to help us with the investigation."

Jordan was speechless. Working with civilians on live cases was a strict no-no; working with a victim's parent was unthinkable. Jordan could feel a numbness spreading across his brain. If the suggestion had been made by a rank-and-file member of the force Jordan would have been laughing his socks off, but this was a Deputy Commissioner speaking. Had there been a major shift of Garda policy that he'd missed -- a shift into Wonderland? If so, he'd missed the memo.

A tall, balding man close to retirement age, O'Malley was Jordan's only real friend in the upper echelons of the force. He was also the only senior garda officer that Jordan fully trusted. Jordan thought that, with his engaging personable manner, O'Malley would have done well as a financial consultant, if he hadn't joined the Guards; either that or a stand-up comedian.

Quigley said, "What has he said so far?"

Jordan blinked to put his mind back in gear and replied, "Nothing of value."

"But you're still holding him, right?"

"He hasn't been released yet. I am hoping that he may provide some useful intelligence when we speak with him again."

"So why aren't you grilling the bastard right now?"

Deadpan, Jordan replied, "Because I don't have the gift of bilocation."

Throwing a glare at Jordan, Deputy Commissioner O'Malley coughed and said, "What Inspector Jordan means to say is that these things can't be rushed."

"I understand," said Quigley. "He's cooling his heels in a cell somewhere. Am I right?" He continued without waiting for a reply, "This man, these offenders. I take it they have a history of... of this sort of offence?"

"They are on the register of sexual offenders, yes," said Jordan.

Quigley seemed to shrink, to crumble. He turned to stare at his own reflection in the window.

"Can we get you something, Shane," said the DC, giving Jordan the dead eye again. "A glass of water, maybe."

Quigley waved a hand at him. "I'd much rather your inspector tell it like it is, Rory. I know there's no point picking up jay Walkers. So what's the plan?"

Rory?

"The search continues. Meanwhile we are looking at individual offenders--"

DC O'Malley chipped in, "As I said earlier, every available man we have is combing the country. All Garda leave has been cancelled and the army is standing by--"

Quigley spun on his heel to face the DC. "Standing by! Standing by? What's the point of that? Why aren't they out searching? Back home, the National Guard would have been called out by now."

Jordan said, "The army will be used at the right time, sir."

"What does that mean?" Quigley snapped. "Right now would be the right time, seems to me. Have you any idea how it feels to have a daughter kidnapped? Have you?"

O'Malley chipped in here. "The answer to that is 'yes', Shane. DI Jordan's own daughter was missing for a week earlier this year."

Lucy was 19 at the time. Jordan knew exactly how it felt, but he could only imagine how much more painful the experience would have been if Lucy had been as young as Emily.

DC O'Malley said, "Inspector Jordan has a lot of experience, Shane. You're going to have to trust him to do his job."

Jordan said, "The army can be a little heavy-handed. Our own search methods are more discreet."

"Discreet! Who needs discreet? What we need is to flush these deviants out of the woodwork and find Emily before... before they... before..." He stuttered to a halt like a locomotive running out of steam.

Jordan said, "It's important not to spook the kidnappers."

"Kidnappers? You think there might be more than one?"

"That is our hope," said Jordan, flying by the seat of his pants. "The more there are the better chance we have. With a group we have the prospect of a split, which can only help us."

Jordan moved to the door and grabbed the handle. "Just one thing before you go," he said. "I understand that Emily was issued with a US passport, recently. We would like to see it. If you could call my office, I'll arrange for an officer to collect it from your house."

"What the fuck d'you want that for? 'Scuse my French." said Quigley.

"We need to be sure that Emily hasn't left the country."

Quigley took a step toward Jordan, balling his fists. "If that's an example of your methods, buster, then God help us." He stepped out of the room, turned and hissed at Jordan, "See that you keep me informed every step of the way or I'll have your badge."

Chapter 11

Quigley slammed the door, leaving the walls trembling.

The Deputy Commissioner said, "I know what you're going to say, Ben, but do what you can to keep him in the loop."

"The loop--?"

"He is the girl's father, after all. He's entitled to be kept informed." O'Malley closed his eyes and pinched the bridge of his nose. "Give him nothing that could jeopardize the investigation, obviously, but throw him a bone now and then."

Jordan said, "I'll tell him as much as I would tell any father, no more and no less."

"That's all I'm asking," said O'Malley.

"And what about his offer of help?"

"Let him down gently. Be diplomatic. Stress the differences between our methods and those of the NYPD. With any luck we'll be able to return his daughter to him before he starts an international firestorm. I hear you've already made progress on the case."

"What've you heard?" said Jordan.

"I've heard there was a sighting of a white van. And I heard that Liam Flood's on board."

Jordan returned to his seat. "You've read my letter of resignation?"

DC O'Malley picked the letter up as if it carried the rabies virus and tossed it across his desk. "If you're serious about it, it should be addressed to Superintendent Briscoe of ODU."

"Briscoe hates my guts. He'd just take it as some sort of admission of guilt, of failure."

"And isn't that what it is, an admission of failure?"

"Your failure, not mine," Jordan said. "Briscoe's given me bugger all to do. How did you expect me to react?"

"How's your health, Ben?"

"I'm still dry, if that's what you mean."

O'Malley was silent for several moments. Then he said, "You can't be serious about this, Ben. If you leave early you won't get the full pension, or anything like it. What age are you? Forty-two? You have many good years ahead of you. The force needs men like you."

"What? As desk jockeys?"

"I'll see that you get posted to a front-line unit."

"When? You've left me in limbo for eight months." Jordan got to his feet. "And you know as well as I do, there's not a division or a station in the country that'll take me on. I've had it. At this stage it's get out or lose my mind."

"That's nonsense, Ben."

"Why did you give me this job?"

"You know how important it is that we find Emily Carter and get her back to her parents unharmed. And you know how highly I think of you. You're the only one I could trust to lead this one."

"Kind words butter no parsnips."

"Find Emily and your good name will be restored, Ben. Don't you see? This is your chance to redeem yourself."

"Didn't know I needed redemption," Jordan said.

"You know as well as I do what the men think of you. They think you're all washed up, a spent force. This is your chance -- your last chance -- to prove them wrong. But fail and you won't need a letter of resignation. They'll demand your head on a platter."

Jordan got up to go.

O'Malley said, "Keep a close eye on Flood. He can be a loose cannon at times. He has... issues."

"Issues?"

"He's our youngest ever DI. His success rate in DV has been phenomenal, unprecedented. But he worries me. He seems to have no life outside the job. He's the most single-minded officer I've ever worked with, completely dedicated to the job, passionate about it. Sometimes I wish I had a hundred men like him. I've offered to move him to other divisions, the Special Detective Unit, Organised Crime, but he refuses to move. I don't understand why, and when I don't understand my men, that makes me nervous."

"So you want me to baby-sit your child prodigy. Is that it?"

"I want you -- and Liam Flood -- to find Emily Carter. That's what I want. And I want you to tear up this letter."

Jordan picked up the letter, folded it, and put it in his pocket. "I'll find Emily. Then we'll talk about this again."

Chapter 12

DI Flood was not at his desk. Jordan asked Garda Walescu where he was.

"He's with Green in Interview Room 1."

"Alone?"

Walescu held her palms upward in a gesture of hopelessness. "I offered to sit in, but he--"

Jordan turned and sprinted to the staircase. He took the stairs to the ground floor at full tilt. The door to Interview Room 1 was locked. He banged on it. No answer. He hammered on it. Still no answer. He stepped into the observation room. Flood was holding Green up against a wall with one hand, beating him about the head and body with the other. Jordan opened the intercom.

"Let me in." No response. "It's Jordan. Let me in."

He returned to the door and hammered on it some more. Flood opened it and Jordan pushed past him.

Green was on his backside propped against the wall, gasping for air, bleeding from around his nose and mouth. He looked semiconscious.

Jordan used his mobile phone to contact Sergeant Payne. "I need a doctor in Interview Room 1, quick as you can. Peter Green needs attention. In the meantime, send someone down to keep an eye on him."

Jordan pushed Flood into the corridor and closed the door.

"Jesus, Liam, what have you done?"

Flood made no answer. His right hand was wrapped in a dish cloth stained with blood.

"What the fuck's the matter with you? Didn't they teach you anything in Templemore? You know you can't question a witness without a second garda in attendance. And you can never beat a prisoner."

Flood's eyes flashed anger. "He's a total piece of shit."

"Green isn't even a prisoner. He hasn't been arrested or even cautioned. What gives you the right to treat him like a punch bag?"

"We need a break in the case, Ben. Green's been playing us. He knows something. I'm sure of it."

"You can't know that."

"So -- what? You want to keep asking him pretty questions, wasting precious time?" Flood ran a sleeve across his forehead.

"There are procedures. People have rights. You can't just rewrite the rule book anytime you want to."

"You think we have time for rules and procedures?"

"And you think beating Green is going to help us find the girl?"

"He knows something," said Flood. "He's holding out on us."

"You don't know that."

"I'm sure of it. I can smell it on him."

Jordan took a step forward. "What is that Zen shit? You can smell it on him. Are you crazy, Liam?"

"Give me five more minutes in there with him, Ben. I was that close. I know he'll give us something."

Jordan grabbed the lapels of Flood's jacket. Up close, he could smell Flood's sweat. "You are crazy. Get back to your desk while I see what can be salvaged from this situation." Jordan pushed him toward the stairs and Flood left. Jordan filled a cup with water from a water cooler, took a deep breath, and stepped inside the interview room.

Green had slumped to the floor. He was now lying on his side, groaning. There was blood smeared on the wall where Flood had held him.

Jordan put the water on the table and helped Green to his feet.

"He just went crazy! He could have killed me," Green said, his lungs gurgling. "I have bad lungs and a weak heart, and he knows that."

Jordan brushed dust from Green's jacket and lowered him onto his seat.

"What did I do to deserve that?" he said.

Jordan replied, "It's vital that we get an early lead in this case."

"Why take it out on me? I know nothing about the child."

"Are you sure about that?"

Green wiped the blood from his lips.

Pushing the cup within Green's reach, Jordan sat on Green's side of the table. "You may know something that you're not aware of."

"Like what?" Green grabbed the cup with a trembling hand and gulped the water down, spilling half of it on the table.

"You may know the names of people we should be talking to, people who enjoy the company of young girls."

Green stared directly at Jordan. "If I had any information, don't you think I would have given it to that -- that other officer?" He made the word sound like an obscenity.

Jordan regarded Green solemnly for a couple of moments. "Well, I'm sorry," he said.

"What d'you mean? What are you saying?" Green's eyes showed extreme alarm.

"He's waiting outside," said Jordan. "I told him you probably knew nothing, but he's not convinced."

"Tell him again," Green whispered. "Tell him I know nothing."

"All right," said Jordan. "I'll try."

Jordan left and locked the door. He lit a cigarette and smoked it down to the butt before re-entering the room. Green hadn't moved. He sat at the table clutching the empty plastic cup.

"I'm sorry," Jordan said. "I tried, but I haven't been able to convince him. He wants to have another word with you."

Green shot to his feet. He shouted through a ragged cough, "You bastards! You have no right--" At this point he was overcome by a coughing fit that lasted two minutes. Jordan fetched a second cup of water from the cooler and handed it to him. Green drank some and his coughing subsided. He said, "You can't treat people like this. I have rights."

Jordan breathed his tobacco breath into Green's face. "What about Emily Carter? Doesn't she have any rights?"

Green's voice faltered. "I know nothing about the girl."

"But you could give us the name of someone who does."

Green blinked.

Jordan produced his pack of cigarettes, shook one out and handed it to Green.

"Thanks," said Green. "You have my matches."

"You were going to give me a name."

"You'll get that other bastard off my case?" Green said.

Jordan produced the matches and handed them over. "Of course."

Chapter 13

They headed south along the coast road to Shankill. The snow was falling in earnest now, big sticky flakes drifting down like tiny parachutes from a solid grey blanket overhead.

"I don't recall the name," said Jordan. "What did he do?"

"Budgie Bolger's a pervert," said Flood. "That's all you need to know." He glanced at Jordan and added, "He's out of prison a while. Maybe five years. I can't remember the specifics."

Bolger's was on a council estate, and it had all the signs of it. All the houses had been painted recently in the same off-white, and the front gardens was all neatly laid out with low-growing shrubs littered with empty cans and crisp packets.

The door was opened by a tall, muscular woman wearing a serious black eye and a housecoat. Somewhere in the house the song Take my Breath Away was playing. Jordan froze. That song had been a favourite of his mother's.

"Mrs. Bolger?" said Flood, showing his ID. "We're here to talk to Budgie."

She ran her eyes over DI Flood, a ghastly half-leer on her face. "Hullo again, Sonny-Jim."

"Get Budgie, Nancy," Flood said, tight-lipped.

She half-closed the door. "Why can't yous leave him alone? He's served his sentence, been a model citizen since they let him out. You know he hasn't had so much as a parking ticket in the past six years."

Flood said, "We just need to ask him a few questions--"

"He's not here. Out wi'h his mates. Won't be back for hours." She began to push the door closed, but Flood's boot kept it open.

"Who is it, Nancy?" a voice called from behind her.

The door opened wide and Jordan got his first look at Budgie Bolger. He was short -- maybe five six -- in his mid-fifties with a shock of white hair and the nose of a serious drinker. His right leg was in plaster from toe to thigh, and he was leaning on an aluminium crutch, standard hospital issue. "What do you want?" he said.

"We have some questions," Flood said.

"All right, ask your bloody questions." Bolger positioned his frame squarely in the doorway. Mrs Bolger stood directly behind him. She towered head and shoulders over him.

The song ended, snapping Jordan back to the present. "Where were you this afternoon between two and four?" he said.

"He was here wi'h me," said Mrs Bolger.

"Right here," said Bolger.

"Can anybody else confirm that?" Flood said to Bolger.

"I told yous, he was wi'h me."

"Anyone apart from your wife," said Flood.

"No, we were alone," said Mrs Bolger.

"What happened to your leg?" Jordan asked.

"He's after fallin' off a roof," said Mrs Bolger. "Not that it's any of your business."

Bolger half-turned to his wife. "Shut up, woman. Go boil some eggs or something."

Nancy Bolger snorted and withdrew.

"I fell off a roof," said Bolger.

"What were you doing on the roof?" said Flood.

"Rescuing a cat from a tree. I tried to reach him from an asbestos roof on an old warehouse. The roof broke. I fell through it. It's a long story."

Right on cue a fat black cat arrived from inside the house and rubbed its deep-pile fur against Bolger's plaster.

"He could've been killed," shouted Mrs Bolger from somewhere in the house.

"When did this happen?" Jordan asked.

"About t'ree weeks ago. End of November."

"Thank you," said Jordan as he and Flood turned to leave.

Nancy Bolger's voice called, "Now feck off and leave us alone."

Jordan said, "That was quite a shiner. Does Bolger have a history of domestic violence?"

"And some!" said Flood. "Nancy spends half her time in A&E. Budgie's very free with his fists."

"But she's six inches taller than him." Jordan shook his head in amazement. "Has she ever registered a complaint about him?"

"Never. I've tried to persuade her, but she makes excuses for him. He had a traumatic childhood in an orphanage, can't help himself. You know the sort of bullshit."

"She seemed to have a soft spot for you," Jordan said, smiling. "You could be in there if you played your cards right."

Flood said, "What happened to you back there, Ben?"

"Nothing. That song. My mother loved it. She played it all day one Monday in September 1986. The cancer took her on the Friday."

They climbed into the car and Jordan used the on-board computer link to PULSE, the Garda computer database, to pull Bolger's file.

Billy Bolger, known as 'Budgie', born February 4, 1950. Raised in St Benedict's orphanage in Brittas. Convicted of indecency eight years earlier, served just 13 months of a three-year sentence. Nothing since.

"It lists a bricklayer called Adam O'Reilly as his only known associate," said Jordan.

"Doesn't surprise me. We should pay O'Reilly a visit. He's another nasty rock spider and he's on my list."

Jordan raised an eyebrow. "Rock spider?" He wasn't familiar with the term.

"They like little cracks. It's an Aussie expression."

Jordan's stomach heaved. "That's pretty disgusting," he said.

Chapter 14

O'Reilly's address was in Blanchardstown, a raw new suburb to the northwest. As Flood drove, Jordan took him to task over his treatment of Green. Jordan had served with men who relished getting down and dirty with suspects and under several senior officers who turned a blind eye to what was euphemistically called 'the direct approach', but he never had the stomach for it. The policing methods used by the modern Garda force were much more enlightened and many of the old guard, who initially scorned the namby-pamby approach, had to admit that the softly-softly approach did work.

Flood was unrepentant. "It produced results, didn't it?"

"The guy has a bad heart. You heard his lungs. What if he'd died?"

"If my auntie had balls she'd be my uncle," said Flood, with a grin.

"I'm serious, Liam. You know your feet wouldn't touch the ground if I reported what happened in that interview room today."

"You're not going to report it, though, are you?"

"Don't ever try anything like that again. This is my investigation. If you want to stay on the case you'll do things my way, okay?"

"Okay."

"I mean it. You'll get no second chance from me."

They stopped at a mobile food van, grabbed a couple of pastrami rolls and coffees to go. The snowfall had intensified, and they ate in the car with the heater running.

Jordan said, "How long've you been an inspector?"

"Not long. Eighteen months."

"You must be the youngest DI on the force."

"I suppose. I was fast-tracked."

"Why?"

"I get results," said Flood, tomato ketchup running down his chin.

Jordan asked what had led Flood to join the force.

"My dad was a copper. I suppose it's in my blood."

"Was?" said Jordan. "Is he retired?"

Flood looked away. "He's been dead for five years."

"Sorry to hear that, Liam. Had you graduated by then?"

"Yes, I was in the force by then. He saw me in my uniform just the once."

"What was his name?" said Jordan. "Would I have known him?"

"Dominic Flood. He served in the North Central Division."

Jordan didn't know the name, but there were hundreds of guards in stations all over the country that he'd never met.

Flood peered into the remnants of his pastrami roll. "He committed suicide. Suffered from depression. He had a difficult childhood."

"He was abused?"

"He never talked about it, but, yes." This was delivered in a flat tone that told Jordan to drop the subject.

As they got back into the car Jordan checked his watch. It was 7:45 pm. "Nearly five hours since Emily was taken," he said. Flood nodded.

There was nothing remarkable about O'Reilly's house, another typical three-bed semi-detached suburban home in faux red-brick, surrounded by hundreds just like it. It had no garage, and there was a white van of the right size with no markings parked in the short driveway.

Flood knocked on the door. No one answered. The house looked deserted.

Flood said, "Shit! He can't be far away. His van's here."

Jordan said, "Can you smell gas?"

"No."

"Well, I can," said Jordan. "Lives could be at risk. We need to force entry."

"Right. You're right. I can smell gas."

They went round the back and peered through the windows. Then Jordan broke a glass panel in the back door, opened it and they stepped inside.

Jordan checked the ground floor; Flood checked upstairs.

In the living room Jordan found slight signs of a struggle, an office chair overturned, a twist in a loose rug, a few papers scattered on the floor.

The van was locked, and the keys were nowhere to be found. Jordan had no trouble getting the driver's door open, but the rear doors were more of a challenge. They could be sprung easily enough, but not without causing damage, compromising the evidence chain. Flood climbed over the seats and opened the door from the inside.

Jordan directed his flashlight inside the van. It was empty.

"Nothing here," said Flood.

"Don't you think that's strange?" said Jordan. "This guy's a bricklayer. Shouldn't there be something? Tools, at least?"

They secured the rear doors of the van and Jordan rang Harcourt Square to organise an impound order for the vehicle.

While they waited for the tow truck, Flood rang the office to bring the team up to date. Then Jordan and Flood went back inside O'Reilly's house and took another look around the ground floor.

A fancy colour printer and a desktop computer sat on the desk. Flood switched the computer on. It booted successfully, but a message appeared on the screen demanding a password.

Rifling through O'Reilly's papers, Jordan came across a bundle of his payslips, each one headed 'Glenmask Enterprises'. The latest one was a week old.

"That's Dinny Kenny's company, isn't it?" said Flood. Dinny Kenny was one of the new breed of super-rich developers that crawled fully-grown from the womb of the 'Celtic Tiger', Ireland's sudden economic renaissance. One of Dublin's richest men, he had building sites all over the city.

Chapter 15

On the fifth floor in the shell of a high-rise building, two men stood face to face. A chill wind blew through the gaping holes in the structure, creating miniature twisters of snowflakes and concrete dust that danced around their legs. To the south-west, towering over a sea of grey-slated roofs, sprinkled with white, the superstructure of the new Aviva stadium poked its fingers of steel into the sky like the chrysalis of some giant moth.

The younger man wore a building worker's hard hat and a donkey jacket that struggled to contain his extended belly. He stamped his feet and blew into his hands.

The older man was in his mid-sixties, his trim figure a testament to his status. Dressed in Italian shoes and a full-length black coat with an astrakhan collar, he held a phone in one gloved hand.

"Where is the bastard?" he said, staring at the phone as if it might answer his question. He hit redial and a voice invited him to leave a message. He swore, disconnected, and stuffed the phone into a pocket. "How could he be so fucking stupid? How could you?"

The younger man, avoiding eye contact. "How could we know who she was? Kids of that age all look alike," he said, sulkily, then, "Sorry, boss."

"Where is she?"

"She's in the rental."

"I'll skin him alive when I catch him," said the older man.

Like giant toys, two tall tower cranes sat idle, their hanging chains swinging in the breeze. The younger man dropped his chin and muttered something. Using the toe of his boot he broke a knob of concrete free from the floor and kicked it out over the edge.

"If you've got something to say, say it," said the older man.

"It's nothing... It's just..."

"Spit it out."

"This girl, she could be worth a lot of money, boss."

The older man pulled a pack of cigarettes and a lighter from a pocket. "You think I don't know that?"

The younger man shrugged his shoulders, stretching his donkey jacket further. "I'm just saying. She's a valuable asset."

"What sort of moron are you? A fucking asset she is not. She's nothing but an albatross around our necks, and we need to ship her out as fast as we can." Sheltering his lighter in his hands, he lit a cigar. "Go find the halfwit. Bring him to me so I can slice his ears off. Then we'll decide what to do about the girl."

Chapter 16

The tow truck arrived and removed the van, and Jordan and Flood drove back towards The Square. The city was awash with Christmas lights and teeming with people. It was after 8 pm and yet the Stephen's Green shopping centre and most of the shops in Grafton Street remained open, capitalizing on the growing Christmas frenzy. Here, shoppers had trampled the snow into grey sludge with only a thin strip of white remaining along the foot of the buildings.

Jordan found Garda Walescu in the interview room with Green, her eyes streaming. The room was full of tobacco smoke attempting to mask various more noxious body odours, and making a poor job of it.

Green held a kitchen towel to his nose where blood still seeped.

"Has the doctor seen him?" said Jordan.

"Yes sir. The doctor says he's overweight and he smokes too much, but there's nothing the matter with him."

Jordan told Green he was free to leave.

"I want to make a formal complaint," Green snarled. "That cocksucker beat seven shades of shite outta me. What's his name?"

Jordan said, "You can make a complaint if you like, but do you really want to make an enemy on the force?"

Green grunted. Then he squinted at Jordan through swollen eyelids "Just forget it. I'm free to go, right?"

"Right, but don't leave the neighbourhood. We may want to talk to you again."

Jordan told Walescu to arrange a car to take Green back to his shop, and returned to Flood's office.

Flood had pulled O'Reilly's file from the PULSE computer network and printed it. All the computer system gave them was a miserable three pages of condensed information.

Jordan took the lift to the Criminal Records Office on the third floor, completed a request form and was handed O'Reilly's permanent file. If the Organisation Development Unit had its wicked way, these permanent files would be buried in an underground vault or -- worse still -- shredded, as PULSE consumed and condensed every piece of data. Only the Commissioner stood between the nirvana offered by the IT evangelists and the traditionalists like Jordan, who were uncomfortable without paper records.

Jordan went through O'Reilly's folder, page by page. What he read sent a shiver down his spine.

Adam O'Reilly, date of birth February 4, 1950, a serial sex offender with a predilection for pre-pubescent girls. He had a string of arrests but only two convictions and a total of six years in prison. The psych notes on his file declared him an incurable sexual addict with strong paedophile tendencies, a recidivist and a constant danger to children.

Chapter 17

Shane Quigley stood in his wife's kitchen watching her fall to pieces. Stella had uncorked a second bottle of Pinot Grigio while the first was half-full, and was refilling her glass.

Quigley stood by the fridge watching her. In the 12 years since he'd known her, Stella had always been in control, always decisive, confident in every decision that she made. In all that time, he'd never known her to lose it. Even as one or other of her businesses teetered on the edge of ruin, she always managed to keep her cool, to talk her way out of trouble. Whatever it took, Stella would find a way. Always. Stella was a true leader, a rock that everyone could rely on.

Stella was always in charge. He often marvelled at her capacity to manage every aspect of their daily lives -- the meals they ate, their activities, the friends they chose, even down to the soap they used, their brand of toilet paper, and the colours of the towels in the bathrooms.

In just five hours, since Emily's abduction, a new Stella Carter had emerged. This was a woman at sea without a rudder. She seemed incapable of rational thought. It was as if a vital part of her brain had ceased to function. She had become forgetful, vague, indecisive, unaware of her surroundings and -- suddenly -- a lush. If the house caught fire, he doubted she'd notice. Of the two Stellas, Quigley preferred the control freak.

He said, "Where's Dolores? Aren't we eating today?"

"I sent her home. She was very upset and I'm not hungry."

He opened the fridge door and inspected the contents.

Stella gave him the eye from her breakfast stool perch. She looked like a monstrous bird of prey. He was the prey. "How can you think about food at a time like this?"

"We need to eat, to keep our strength up."

She poured more wine into her glass, spilling some on the counter top. "Our daughter's missing and all you can think about is comfort eating."

Quigley bit his tongue. It seemed to him that food was a better choice of comfort than alcohol.

"Why can't you do something to find her?" she said, waving her glass, spilling more wine.

"Like what, for Pete sake? We've alerted the police. What else can I do?"

"Go find her. Forget about your stomach for once."

"I can't see the point of starving ourselves. Have you any idea how quickly muscle can turn to fat? I need my carbs."

"You're a pig!" she said. "I bet if whatshername asked for something, you wouldn't waste time rummaging in the fridge. She wouldn't have to ask a second time. You'd jump to attention, salute smartly and spring into action."

"She's my agent. Who d'you think brings in those lucrative sponsorship deals every year? Without whatshername, as you call her, I'd have nothing to live on."

"Hah!" she snorted.

He pulled a couple of huge T-bones from the fridge, put a frying pan on the stove, lit the gas and poured in some olive oil. Then he spread the steaks on a chopping board and said, "D'you want one of these?"

"I'm not hungry." She took a slug from her glass.

Quigley began pounding the two steaks with a wooden tenderizer. When he stopped, she said, "I told you I'm not hungry."

"I heard you," he said, dropping both steaks into the pan.

"Pig!" Stella picked up the bottle and left the room. Quigley grabbed the half-empty bottle abandoned by Stella, poured a generous amount of red wine into the pan. The pan welcomed the wine with an excited sizzle. He found a spatula and turned the steaks over. Then he opened the freezer in search of French fries.

Chapter 18

Emily sat against the wall gripping her legs, her knees tucked under her chin. She had missed her evening meal and she was hungry. It was dark. Her watch told her it was close to 9 o'clock, nowhere near her bedtime. She was determined to follow her usual routine as far as she could. She still had her satchel and she would have done her homework if there had been enough light to read by -- and if she had her glasses. She regretted that she wouldn't get to complete her geography project. She and Aimee been working on a project about the famine in Darfur, Sudan. It was nearly finished. Emily had downloaded a lot of information from the Internet and some of it was in her satchel.

She had no idea how long the man would leave her on her own.

She knew her daddy would come to rescue her, and she kept that thought uppermost in her mind. He was searching for her right now and he wouldn't stop until he found her. When my daddy comes, she thought, he will knock seven bells out of the evil man. That was one of her daddy's phrases and Emily liked the sound of it. She could picture the bells spinning around the man's head as her daddy slugged him with his big fists. That was another one of her daddy's words: 'slugged'. She almost smiled.

She had had to use the potty. She held on as long as she could. Now it was nearly full and she knew it would overflow if she had to use it again. She had pushed it as far away from her as she could, but not so far that she couldn't reach it. The smell was pretty bad, but that wasn't the worst part. There was no toilet paper. That was the worst part.

She had shouted herself hoarse, but no one had heard her. The loop in the wall had resisted all her attempts to shift it. She wondered if even her daddy would be strong enough to pull the loop from the wall.

She turned her attention to the chain. It was made from pieces of folded iron too thick for her to bend, but each link had a tiny gap and she tried to prise the ends apart. She wasn't strong enough; they were too heavy. She gave up and resumed her position against the wall.

Chapter 19

The desk in O'Reilly's house gave up its secrets. Jordan found a phone list with an entry that read 'work'. He rang the number.

A man's voice answered, "Adam? Where are you?"

"This is Detective Inspector Jordan. Who am I speaking to?"

"Frank Hughes. Why are you calling from Adam O'Reilly's phone? Is Adam there?"

"He's not here. I need to speak to the site manager."

"That's me," said Hughes "Has something happened to Adam?"

"How do I get to the site? I need to speak to you urgently."

Hughes took a few more moments to absorb that. "I was about to go home, but I'll wait for you here." He gave Jordan directions to the site.

The snowfall had eased, but the air temperature had plummeted, and a sheen of heavy frost clung to the road surfaces. Jordan reduced his speed, and they arrived at the gate of the Glenmask Docklands development shortly before 9:45 pm.

The site gate was locked, and the site looked deserted, although there were lights on everywhere. Two tower cranes stood idle, their chains swinging in the falling snow. Flood pressed the bell on the gate and a gateman appeared. Jordan flashed his badge and the gateman let them in, handing them hard hats before directing them to the site office. They climbed the wooden steps and Jordan opened the door without knocking.

The office was lit by a blinding arc light. A red-faced man with an enormous beer gut hanging over the belt of his jeans stood at a table, staring at a blueprint.

Jordan showed his badge again. "Detective Inspector Jordan. This is Detective Inspector Flood."

Hughes's belly shook as he turned toward them. He offered a callused hand and they each shook it. He said, "So what's so urgent it couldn't wait until the morning?"

Jordan said, "We're looking for Adam O'Reilly."

"That makes three of us," said Hughes. "He was a no-show this morning. I had to draft in a bricky from another site for the day. What's he done?"

"How reliable is he?" asked Jordan.

"We expect a few no-shows most mornings. Guys have heavy nights -- you know -- but we usually have a full complement on payday, and I've never known O'Reilly miss a shift. The money he's on, he'd have to be off his head."

"Give me O'Reilly's mobile number," said Flood.

Hughes found the number on his phone and handed it to Flood. Flood hit the dial button. He got through to voicemail, disconnected, and transferred the number to his own phone.

"Have you any idea where we might find him?" said Jordan.

"Sounds pretty serious." Hughes flashed a perfectly aligned set of dentures. "I have his address on file." He opened a filing cabinet, pulled out a folder and read out O'Reilly's address.

"We've been there," said Flood. "Does he have a girlfriend or any close relatives?"

Hughes stuck his thumbs behind the belt straining to hold the line where his waist should have been. "I wouldn't know."

"You must have a next-of-kin contact for him," said Jordan.

Hughes consulted the file. "It says here O'Reilly's next-of-kin is Dinny Kenny. Doesn't surprise me. Mr Kenny's always been good at looking after his jailbirds."

"The city's biggest developer took on jailbirds?" said Flood.

Hughes dropped the folder back into the cabinet. "Mr. Kenny's famous for taking on ex-cons. The guy has a big heart. There's three on this site, and I know several at other sites."

Flood handed the foreman a card. "Give us a ring as soon as you see O'Reilly."

"What's he wanted for?" said Hughes. "Should I be looking for a permanent replacement?"

Jordan opened the door and stepped onto the raw wood staircase. "Just call us when you see him."

As they returned their hard hats at the gate, Jordan asked the gateman casually how Dinny Kenny got started in the building trade.

"Dinny? No one really knows. He came into the business with a pile of cash."

"I expect he started as a small builder," said Flood to Jordan.

The gateman laughed. "No, not Dinny. He never laid a brick in his life."

"Where did he work before?" said Jordan.

"They say he was the accountant in an orphanage," said the gateman, a glint in his eye.

Flood said, "You mean the bursar."

The gateman had Jordan's full attention. "You think he may have skimmed cash from the orphanage?"

"Like a thief in the night," said Flood.

The gateman held up both hands. "I'm not saying that, Officer. No one's ever accused Dinny of anything, you know. But I'm not the first to wonder."

Chapter 20

Amillionaire many times over and a well-known philanthropist, rumour had it Dinny Kenny had paid over €8 million for his house on Ailesbury Road, a palatial mansion set in an acre of ground and surrounded on all sides by ambassadorial residences.

Jordan rang the intercom at the gate, gave his name and rank and was buzzed onto the property. By the time he'd parked the car and he and Flood had climbed the steps, the front door was open. A uniformed housemaid invited them inside, led them through to a room lined with leather-bound tomes, where Dinny Kenny sat by an open fire, a glass of whiskey in his hand.

Jordan introduced himself and Flood.

"You'll join me?" Kenny said, indicating the whiskey and directing the detectives to two chairs.

"No thank you," said Jordan. "We're on duty."

Kenny was a diminutive man with a bulbous nose. He wore a smoking jacket and Italian shoes. He took a slug from his glass and closed his eyes as he swallowed.

Jordan salivated. He could taste the oily smoothness of the whiskey at the back of his throat. He coughed and began, "I understand that Adam O'Reilly works for you."

"Yes. He's a first rate bricklayer. He's worked for me for several years. Why, what's he been up to?"

"When you say several years...?"

"Ten or eleven. What's this all about, Inspector?"

"We'd like to speak with Mr O'Reilly. Can you tell us where we might find him?"

"I assume he's at home."

"We called to his house and he's not there. We need to speak with him as a matter of urgency."

"You're going to have to tell me what this is about, Inspector. Do I need to call my lawyer?"

"You will be aware that Stella Carter's daughter was abducted earlier today," said Jordan.

Kenny nodded. "It was on the nine o'clock news. I was shocked to hear it. Stella and I are good friends. We've been involved in various charity functions together. Remarkable woman."

Jordan continued, "We suspect that Mr O'Reilly's van may have been used in the kidnapping."

Kenny pursed his lips. "You must be mistaken, Inspector. I can assure you O'Reilly is a completely reformed character. He wouldn't have anything to do with something like that."

Flood had been silent up to this point. Now, through clenched teeth, he said, "No mistake, sir. If you know where we can find O'Reilly, you'd be wise to tell us now."

Kenny put his glass down on a coffee table and rose to his feet. "I don't like your tone, Inspector." He took a phone from his pocket, selected a number and pressed the call button.

Jordan said, "Can you confirm where you were this afternoon, between two and four?"

"You have to be joking, Mr. Jordan." Someone answered the phone. Kenny held up a finger. He stepped from the room and closed the door.

Jordan and Flood had time to exchange no more than a glance before Kenny returned. He handed the phone to Jordan.

"Jordan?" It was Superintendent Lassiter. "What the hell d'you think you're doing?"

"We're doing our job, searching for a missing schoolgirl."

"You have no business with Dinny Kenny. Get out of there. Get to Stella Carter's house. You're needed there."

"We have a couple more questions."

"No you haven't," said Lassiter. "Apologize to Mr Kenny and leave now. That's an order. There's been a development. Declan Fairweather, the journalist, got a call from the IRA Joint Command. They claim to have Emily. They're demanding the release of Robert Crowe."

Robert Emmet Crowe, leader of a fringe dissident group, the Irish Republican Freedom Force, had been caught red-handed and convicted of possession of bomb-making materials four years earlier.

Jordan disconnected and handed the phone back to Kenny. "Are you refusing to say where you were this afternoon, Mr Kenny?"

"My office staff can confirm where I was," said Kenny. "I was at my desk."

Jordan said, "And you've no idea where we might locate O'Reilly?"

Kenny took a quick slug from his glass. "O'Reilly works on the Docklands development. You'll find him there on Monday morning, early."

As Jordan drove toward Stella Carter's house in Stepaside, he filled Flood in on the superintendent's news.

"What the hell is the IRA Joint Command?"

"Never heard of them," said Jordan. "See if you can get Macklin on the phone." Superintendent Macklin was head of the Anti-Terrorist Unit.

Flood made the call. Superintendent Macklin was off duty and it took a few minutes of arguing to wangle his home number. Flood rang Macklin at home. He put the phone on loudspeaker before identifying himself and Jordan and the case they were working on. Then he asked the superintendent about the IRA Joint Command.

Macklin hesitated. "We are aware that such an organisation has been set up," he said, "but this is the first time we've heard from them. I have a team working on it."

"What about the terrorists' demands?" said Flood. "Any chance that Crowe will be released?"

"You know the politicians will never do that, Liam." The government would never release Crowe -- or any prisoner -- under duress. If they did, the flood gates would open. Every Garda graduate fresh out of Templemore knew that.

Flood thanked the superintendent and disconnected.

When Jordan told Flood that Lassiter had said they had no business interviewing Kenny, Flood became quiet. It was too dark to see his face clearly, but the glimpses that Jordan caught in the light from oncoming traffic told him that Flood was fit to be tied.

"Don't worry about it, Liam," said Jordan. "That's just the way the game is played at the top."

"Money talks."

"That's another way of putting it," said Jordan.

"A tree is recognised by its fruit," Flood said.

"What's that supposed to mean?"

"It's from the Gospel of St Matthew." Flood turned his face away from Jordan. "I hate these rich, well-placed men. 'It is easier for a camel to go through the eye of a needle than for a rich man to enter the kingdom of God.'"

"That one I've heard." Jordan laughed.

"If Kenny is involved in Emily's abduction we'll never get him to trial. Men like that have too many friends in high places."

"With strange handshakes and secret signals, you mean?"

"Yes. It's like working with your hands tied and dressed in a straightjacket."

Jordan said, "We've no reason to suppose that he is involved, have we?"

"No, but if we did, he'd probably get off scot free. It's frustrating and I hate it."

"What I find frustrating is that we haven't found Emily. And I hate that she's going to have to spend a night with whatever monster has her."

Chapter 21

Emily was cold and hungry. She couldn't shake the horrible thought that she would be left here in chains; that nobody would ever come back and she would starve to death. 100 years from now her dried-out skeleton would be found by a wrecking crew when they decided to demolish the building, the metal bracelet rusted around the bones of her wrist.

Emily hated being locked up. She hated this house. It had no furniture, not even a TV, and no heating, and it smelled of old. She hated being separated from her parents, and she hated being chained like an animal in the zoo. She hated the man who had grabbed her from her bike. Most of all, she hated the potty. She was nearly 12. It was degrading to be treated like a baby.

Emily dredged her mind and found a lot of information drilled into her from a young age about evil men and the dangers of talking to strangers. She had a lot of warnings, signs to look out for, strategies for self-protection, but no one had ever told her what the evil men would do to her if they caught her. She knew they might kill her, but she had nothing but a vague idea what else they might do.

She thought about her parents; they would be frantic with worry. Her daddy would be really, really angry, grinding his teeth and pile-driving his fists through the walls. She couldn't picture her mother at all. She'd never seen her lose her cool about anything. And she'd never seen her mammy cry. She was always in charge, giving orders, always in control of everything -- even her emotions. She tried to imagine her mammy and her daddy together, talking quietly, comforting one another, but she couldn't.

At 11 o'clock a different man came. This man had a huge tummy that overlapped his belt and looked like it might burst if he took a deep breath. He emptied the potty and gave Emily some food. It was not healthy food -- a miserable, lukewarm hamburger and chips and a bar of chocolate. There was no fruit or vegetables. Emily knew that she needed vegetables for a balanced diet, but she said nothing about this to the man. She wolfed the food down.

When she'd finished the food, she tried talking to him. She complained about the potty, the smell, the toilet paper, the food, the cold and the chains. She demanded that he go back to the laneway and find her glasses. He paid no attention, looking out the window, or watching her eat. She stood up and stamped her feet and shouted at him. She told him what her daddy would do to him when he came. The man ignored her. He collected the food wrappers and left again without a word. Emily felt sad and angry, but she didn't cry. She refused to cry.

Before entering Stella Carter's house, Jordan asked Flood to wait, and made a call to Packie, his friend from Donegal. "How did the move go? I hope you managed without me."

"Oh, sure. Lugging all that furniture up two flights of stairs was no problem. What d'you want?"

"What can you tell me about the IRA Joint Command?" A staunch Republican, now living on a pension, Packie had been a member of the Provisional IRA with no obvious means of support all through the years of the Northern 'Troubles'.

Packie's response was immediate and unequivocal. "Never heard of them. Sounds like someone's wet dream."

Jordan knew when he was being lied to. He knew Packie too well. "Come on, Packie, you can do better than that."

"Sorry, Ben. You know I'm not in the loop anymore."

"You owe me, Packie." A couple of years earlier, the Donegal man had been fitted up by an over-eager member of an anti-subversive unit, and Jordan had made the planted evidence disappear. There was more to it than that, but the bottom line was that he owed Jordan big time.

"Yeah, yeah, I know, but I've become quite attached to my kneecaps over the years."

Jordan waited.

"All right," Packie growled, "I have heard a rumour that the various factions, the Reals, the Continuity and the dregs of the Provos have banded together under one command."

"What about the INLA?"

"Maybe some of them too. But word is it's no more than a talking shop."

"You have the names of any members?"

"Sorry. That's all I have."

"Get me something as soon as you can, Packie. Anything you can find."

"I'll try, but asking those sorts of questions in the wrong bar could seriously damage a person's health."

Jordan terminated the call and Flood rang the Stella-Quigley doorbell.

Chapter 22

When Jordan and Flood arrived at Emily's parents' house, Jordan could see no outward sign that anything unusual was going on, apart from the single unmarked Garda car standing in the driveway beside a Lexus and a VW Golf GTI.

The comparison with his own new house in Sandymount brought a rueful smile to Jordan's lips. This gorgeous architect-designed mansion set in its own grounds, bounded by a stream on one side and woodland on the other, was so way above anything he could aspire to that his own house lost some of its glamour.

They were admitted by a servant girl in her early twenties. She led them to a living room where they found Garda David Irwin hovering around a house telephone connected to a recorder and a portable computer for trace-back.

Irwin completed the briefing started by Superintendent Lassiter. The IRA Joint Command's demands, as conveyed to Fairweather, the newspaperman, were a million euros in used notes and the immediate release of Robert Emmet Crowe.

Ever since his incarceration with three companions in a high security prison, the nationalist activist Crowe had featured in the papers about once every month in one story or another. A vestige of the romanticism of the old republican ideals of yesteryear still clung to these men. And romantic republicanism still sold newspapers.

The kidnappers would call the Carter home number again at seven o'clock in the morning with instructions for the exchange.

Jordan asked if the newspaperman had asked to speak to Emily.

"I don't think so, sir," Garda Irwin replied.

"So we don't know that they have her at all. It could be a simple con. Make sure you ask to speak to Emily if they call back. Make it plain to them that they will get nothing if they cannot prove they have the girl and that she's alive."

#

Stella Carter was in her late thirties, the youngest in a family whose involvement in Irish business dated back to the 1920s. Known as Ireland's Iron Lady, she had proven herself smarter than her father and tougher than all of her siblings. The latest estimates had put her net worth at more than €20 million. Dressed in a crisp grey suit, her hair pulled back from her face and tied in a severe bun, she sat perched on the edge of her seat, eyes downcast, staring at her hands clasped in her lap. The expression on her face could have sunk a battleship, and there were signs of recent tears.

Shane Quigley directed Jordan and Flood to seats.

Jordan felt as if he had joined one of Stella's business meetings and was about to make his sales pitch.

Leaning forward, Quigley peered at Jordan from behind his deep tan. "Tell us what we should be doing, Inspector." That same deep voice and transatlantic accent.

Jordan said, "How quickly can you produce the cash?"

Quigley glanced at Stella before answering, "We have quarter of a million in the house. Finding more will be a serious problem."

"That's not going to be enough," said Jordan.

Stella blanched and covered her face with her hands. Quigley said, "All our assets are tied up in the businesses, Inspector. It could take a week or more to raise a million."

"We can't do it," Stella screamed from behind her hands. Quigley put an arm across her shoulders. She shrugged him off. "We couldn't raise a million. Not in a week, not in a month, not in a million years."

"How much can you raise?" said Flood.

Quigley lifted one huge shoulder. "If we called in all outstanding favours, half a million, maybe."

"You should do that now," said Jordan. "Get as much cash together as you can."

Quigley's colour deepened. "There are pieces of furniture worth more than a million in this house. Heck, Stella's wardrobe is worth twice that. See that picture?" indicating a painting on the wall. "That's a Louis Brennan. An original. Stella paid close to two million for it."

Jordan glanced at the picture. "Two million? For that?" It looked like two old horses under a tree in a fog.

"Could fetch ten million at auction, easy."

"That doesn't help," said Jordan.

Quigley balled his fists again. "Listen, buster. I'm doing the best I can. This is our daughter we're talking about."

Stella shot to her feet. "Stop it! Stop it!" she shouted. "Stop arguing. We need to stay focused."

Quigley said, "You're right, honey. I'm sorry." Then to Jordan, "But what about the kidnappers' other demand?"

Flood answered him, "That could be a problem. There's no way the government is going to make any concessions to the IRA."

Quigley sprang to his feet. "What are you saying? It's hopeless? Even if we could raise a million we won't get Emily back? Is that what you're saying?"

Jordan threw a look at Flood before answering, "No, no, that's not what we're saying. Not at all. What Inspector Flood means is that we'll have to find a way to negotiate our way around that problem when the time comes."

Stella had listened quietly to this exchange. Now she lifted her chin. Her expression hardened and a determined gleam appeared in her eyes. She snapped her fingers at Quigley. He handed her a mobile phone. She made a call and left the room, saying, "Austin, this is Stella Carter..."

Austin Daly was Minister for Justice. Flood suppressed a groan.

"So, how's our investigation going, guys?" said Quigley.

Our investigation.

Flood opened his mouth, said nothing and closed it again.

"We are chasing several leads," said Jordan. "Was there something specific you wanted to ask us?"

"What about that pervert you had in custody earlier? Is he still there? Did you manage to squeeze anything out of him? And what can you tell me about this Joint Command, terrorist group?"

"Those are police matters," said Flood.

"Sure, I understand that," Quigley said. "But my role has been cleared at the highest possible level."

"Your role?" said Jordan.

"I have some experience," said Quigley. "I'm a resource. You can use me as you see fit. Give me small jobs to do. Heck, send me out to Starbucks, I won't mind."

Jordan said, "You worked on kidnap cases with the NYPD? Hostage negotiation, maybe?"

Quigley broke eye contact with Jordan, directed his gaze towards Flood. "To be honest, guys, I never actually served with the PD. I flunked the Academy, but I completed almost all the training."

Speechless, both Jordan and Flood looked at the large American for a few moments. Then Flood said, "When you say your role has been cleared at the highest level, what are we talking about? The Deputy Commissioner?"

"Higher than that," he said.

"The Minster for Justice?" said Jordan.

"Higher than that."

Jordan said, "Leave us your cell phone number, and Ms Carter's." Quigley wrote the two numbers on a scrap of paper and handed it to Jordan.

As Jordan and Flood got into their car, Flood said, "I don't have time for this bullshit, Ben. Isn't there some way we can get him off our backs?"

"You heard him," said Jordan, grimly. "He has clearance from the highest level."

"I don't care where he gets his clearance from. I don't want him getting under my feet."

Chapter 23

Garda Walescu was waiting for them at the main entrance to The Square, her eyes shining with excitement. "I've done some checking," she said, "and St Benedict's Orphanage, where Bolger was brought up, is owned by Dinny Kenny's development company -- Glenmask Enterprises."

Flood gave her a blank look. "So what? It's derelict. Has been for years." He pressed the button to summon the lift.

Walescu gave Flood a withering look and handed a file to Jordan. One glance at the news clippings inside and the stories came flooding back. The place was built in the 1930s, and closed its doors in 1984, the year he graduated from Templemore. Hundreds of children had received merciless treatment at the hands of those entrusted with their wellbeing. The truth that emerged was of a children's hell; the place had been run for decades as a sort of activity holiday resort for paedophiles. Children as young as three were subjected to physical, emotional and sexual torment at the hands of heartless monsters, and the abuse went on for years. Some children did not survive the experience. Excavations of the grounds at the back of the building had uncovered dozens of skeletons.

Jordan shuddered. "God, I remember," he said. Distant echoes from his own childhood bubbled up in his mind like sheep's eyes in mutton soup. After 12 years with the Christian Brothers he had emerged relatively unscathed, but the daily trepidation of seeing the brothers' merciless treatment of his classmates and the ever-present threat of corporal punishment had left their scars. He often wondered why he had avoided the worst of the beatings and he put it down to the brothers' respect for his musical ability, which was apparent from a young age. They often referred to his prodigious natural talent as 'a gift from God' and must have had an inbuilt reluctance to interfere with it by damaging his hands with leather or stick.

Walescu said, "Shouldn't we check it out, sir? Emily could be there."

Jordan closed the file, gave it back to Walescu and said to Flood, "She's right, Liam, we should check it."

Speaking in a monotone, Flood said, "Let the little children come to me and do not hinder them, for the Kingdom of God belongs to such as these." The lift door opened, and he stepped inside. Jordan and Walescu remained where they were, open-mouthed. Flood turned to face them and added, "Mark Chapter 10, verse 14."

Jordan said, "We should check it out, Liam."

"Wild goose chase," said Flood, and the lift door slid closed.

Jordan said, "We'll need a warrant, Mary."

Walescu fished a piece of paper from the file. "I have one already."

"Full marks for initiative," said Jordan. "Can you come with me? Are you free to leave your desk?"

"Yes, sir."

"Right, let's go," said Jordan, making for his car. Garda Walescu followed him, taking three steps for every two of Jordan's.

They drove north for five miles on the M1 before turning off the motorway and into a maze of country roads. Two miles outside the village of Brittas, near a half-built estate, they found St Benedict's Orphanage. A massive, brooding run-down redbrick building, its front door boarded up, it sat grimly behind high walls and wrought-iron gates. Above the door on the concrete fascia were the words: 'The Home For Lost Children'.

The gate was padlocked and carried a sign that read: "BEWARE GUARD DOGS". A smaller sign read: "PRIVATE. This building is the property of Glenmask Enterprises. For emergencies or enquiries ring..." Jordan recognized the site manager Frank Hughes's number.

Three guard dogs barred their way, watching them silently as if daring them to enter. Jordan rang the number and Hughes answered. Jordan told him that they required immediate entry to the building.

"There's no power. It's late. You won't be able to see anything," said Hughes. "I'll meet you there first thing in the morning."

"Now," said Jordan. "We have flashlights."

"It's been locked up for years. There's nothing in there."

"Secure these dogs and open the building right now," said Jordan. "If you don't I'll call out the cavalry and the dogs'll be shot."

By the time Hughes joined them, 20 minutes later, the wind had got up and the temperature had plummeted. Hughes glared at Jordan before opening the gate and tying the barking dogs to a retaining bar.

"Quiet!" he yelled, and the dogs fell silent. Hughes opened the building.

Jordan and Walescu switched on their flashlights and stepped inside. The smell of mould and dry rot hit them right away, but the windows all looked secure. As they moved from room to room, a deep melancholy seized Jordan's heart. He climbed the stairs, and counted 27 rooms on three floors, all devoid of furniture. He visited every one of them. The place was empty and silent. Cast iron hoops set into the walls in some of the upstairs rooms were the only physical vestiges of the building's horrific past, and yet the ghosts of the place seemed to echo all around him.

On his way out he opened the door to the space under the stairs and was confronted by an old-fashioned traveller's chest sitting on cracked linoleum. He checked inside the chest, disturbing several spiders. It was full of old curtains, brass curtain rails, and dusty pieces of carpet.

It was only when he exited the building that Jordan realized Walescu hadn't stayed the course. He found the young garda in the car, flushed and sweating: classic signs of a panic attack.

"What did you find, sir?" she asked.

"Nothing. What happened to you?"

Walescu waved a hand at him. "I'm sorry, sir, the place gave me the horrors. I'll be all right in a minute."

Jordan warmed to the young garda. Her response to the house of horrors did her credit. Jordan's own reaction had been visceral, but controlled; the more severe effect of the place on Walescu reflected her youth and lack of experience. Jordan knew too many men on the force who would have been unmoved by that building. This young woman cared.

Walescu said nothing more about the episode on the way back to base, and Jordan put it from his mind.

Chapter 24

Three men stood on the ground floor in the shell of a high-rise building. One was tall, dark-skinned with a full head of grey hair and a bushy moustache, like a Turk. The second looked like an elf or a leprechaun, diminutive, with almost no hair and tiny, piercing eyes. He held a photograph close to his face. Dinny Kenny, the developer, was there too, wearing his Italian shoes and the leather coat with the astrakhan collar, a phone glued to his ear. The snow was falling again, a freezing wind howling through the gaping holes in the structure.

Kenny said, "I have a bid of thirty on the phone."

"Thirty-five," said the small man.

The Turk snatched the photograph from him and studied it for a couple of seconds. "How old did you say she was?"

"Eleven," said Kenny.

"She looks older," said the elf.

The Turk made a bid. "Forty."

Kenny spoke into the phone. "Yuri? I have a bid of forty thousand."

"Forty-five," shouted the small man.

"Hold on, Yuri. Are there any more bids? Otto?"

The Turk shook his head, and Kenny spoke into the phone again. Then he said to the small man, "Forty-seven thousand on the phone."

Furious, the small man made a dismissive gesture with his hands. "Forget it," he snarled.

The two under-bidders staked off, and Kenny spoke into the phone again. "She's yours, Yuri. When d'you want us to deliver?" He waited for the reply before disconnecting and making another call. "Have you found him yet?" Then, "Keep looking. Ring me when you find him, day or night. Yuri won the auction. We'll need to ship her out tomorrow on the noon ferry. In the meantime, move her to the studio. We'll do a quick photo-shoot in the morning. Tell the others to get there early: we'll start at seven-thirty."

Chapter 25

Jordan dropped Walescu off at the city centre and went on to The Square. It was 11 pm. Apart from Sergeant Payne, the Incident Room on the third floor was deserted. The sergeant had removed his tie and loosened his collar, and was devouring a double beef-burger with all the trimmings.

"Still here, Sergeant?" said Jordan. "Don't you have a home to go to?"

The sergeant wiped his mouth. "Sorry, Inspector. I haven't eaten all day. I was waiting to update you."

"Shoot," said Jordan.

"House-to-house enquiries produced very little, apart from the white van sightings and reports of unrest in the Carter-Quigley household."

"Oh? What sort of unrest?"

"Domestic stuff. Doors slamming, raised voices, cars moving around in the middle of the night, going back over several years. Nothing concrete, but I'd say they're not the model household they'd like everyone to believe."

"Okay, better follow that up in the morning. Anything else? Anything from the school?"

"Emily has a lot of friends. She's a popular young lady. And she's perfectly happy at home, as far as we could tell. We had quite a good response to the appeal. Did you catch it?"

"No."

"It was on the nine o'clock news. I expect they'll repeat it on the late news bulletin. There were sightings of Emily all over the country and even some in other countries -- Spain and France. There was one sighting in Nigeria!"

"Anything useful from that lot?"

"Nothing much. We're following up on a few. Also, I spoke with the Anti-Terrorist Unit. They have nothing on the IRA Joint Command, but one of the names of ex-employees that Ms Carter came up with -- Tom Dwyer -- is a suspected republican sympathiser."

"Do we have anything on him?"

"He has a juvenile record. Nothing heavy." He handed Jordan the file.

Jordan walked to the South Circular Road. Ben and Kate Jordan had two homes in Dublin. When they moved from their Georgian townhouse on the SCR to a modern detached house in the fashionable suburb of Sandymount, Kate's income as a medical consultant had made it possible to retain both houses. The rocketing price of property was the main rationale for this, but the possibility of a marital schism was another that lurked in the backs of their minds. The old house was no more than three-quarters of a mile from Harcourt Square, and since his last ill-advised bout of drinking, it had become Ben's lonely bachelor pad.

The snow lay thick and treacherous underfoot. It had stopped falling, but a biting wind from the river had coated the surface with an icy crust.

The clock tower in Rathmines rang the half hour as Ben stepped into his local bar to catch the last TV news bulletin of the day. Standing in front of a massively blown-up picture of Emily, Stella Carter appeared in an appeal recorded from the 9 o'clock News. Dressed in a powder-blue suit, she started firm, resolute, upbeat, optimistic, a strong-willed member of the business community, but within a few seconds she had crumbled, sobbing, into the distraught mother that she also was. Tight-lipped, Shane Quigley completed the appeal, speaking with a slight tremor in his soft American accent, his words of entreaty laced with the slightest hint of a hidden threat.

"Give Emily back to us unharmed and we will try to forget that this ever happened. Emily's only eleven. She has her whole life ahead of her. She's a United States citizen. The USA doesn't take kindly to mistreatment of its citizens. Give us back our daughter."

Speak softly, but carry a big stick, thought Jordan.

Stella added "Please, please," between sobs.

The cameras switched to the Deputy Commissioner, Rory O'Malley, who provided a more direct threat to the kidnappers.

"Let me say this to the kidnappers: Give up this child now, before any harm is done. Be warned that every resource at the disposal of the State has been mobilized to find Emily and return her to her family. We will search every house, every farmhouse, every byre and outhouse in the country until we find this child. No stone will be left unturned. We will find her. There is nowhere on this island that you can hide. Release Emily now. Tonight. If Emily is released unharmed I will recommend leniency, but if any harm comes to her you will face the full rigors of the law."

"Strong stuff," said the barman. "Can I get you another one of those?" pointing to Jordan's tomato juice. "Or something stronger, maybe?"

Jordan was tempted, but he was determined never to fall off the wagon again. No, he would remain teetotal until he found Emily or hell froze, whichever came first, and no matter what life chucked at him.

The trial separation had happened so suddenly, so rapidly that Jordan had nothing in the old house but a change of clothes and a few sticks of furniture that were left behind when they moved. Top of the list of his personal problems, second only to the pain of separation from his wife and daughter, was the loss of contact with his beloved piano. Ripping into his jazz repertoire provided him with a release from the burden of his work.

As he stepped in through the door he rang Kate. He got Kate's voicemail and left a short message: "Call me. We need to talk."

Then he rang his daughter. Lucy picked up right away. "Hi Dad. Where are you?"

"I'm over in the South Circular," he said. "Have you seen your mother today?"

"Not yet, Dad. She's been delayed at the hospital."

"How's college?"

"Busy. We have exams. It's been a bit overwhelming, to be honest."

"You'll do fine," he said. "You have your mother's brains."

She laughed. "And your looks. Just my luck!"

"Everything okay with you, love?"

"I'm fine," she said. "You've no need to worry about me, Dad. Look after your own problems. I told you before I only ever experimented with the drugs."

There was no answer to this. Jordan had a number of graphic pictures of Lucy tucked away in his memory. Lucy lying senseless in a squat, strung out on heroin, a syringe in her arm, Lucy with her head in the toilet, puking her insides out, Lucy with red rings around her eyes, recovering in hospital...

The conversation rattled on for a while, Lucy's tone laced with exaggerated cheer. But the angst in her voice was unmistakeable.

After the call he put a TV dinner in the microwave and opened the file that Sergeant Payne had given him.

Tom Dwyer, aged 29, a personal trainer with Stella Carter's 'Sweat Box' company for two years before being dismissed for petty theft. He had spent six months in Shanganagh Castle young offenders' detention centre in 1990. Nothing since, although he'd been picked up by Scotland Yard and questioned about possible IRA associations and activities in London. The British authorities hadn't charged him with anything.

It was midnight before Jordan checked his mailbox. There was just one long, ominous-looking manila envelope in there, delivered by courier. Jordan knew what it was before he opened it, but still the sight of the contents took his breath away. He threw the divorce papers across the room and climbed the stairs.

Chapter 26

Emily awoke with a start. There was a flashlight on the ground and the man was fiddling with the iron shackle on her wrist. She gave a yelp and pulled her arm away. She could barely see him, it was so dark, but she knew this was the man who'd given her the food. She recognized his strange smell. Her hands became fists, clutched against her chest. She said, "What are you doing?" It was all she could manage.

He said, "Give me your arm."

Emily said, "Why?"

He gave no answer, and for some reason she was reminded of the time she had her tonsils removed. The doctor had injected her and told her to count backwards from ten. She'd asked why, and got no answer. The next thing she knew she was lying in bed with a sore throat, and her daddy was beside the bed, smiling, and telling her the operation was over.

The man grabbed her arm and held onto it so tightly that it hurt. Emily complained. He unlocked the manacle, tied her hands behind her back and covered her mouth with the sticky tape as the first man had done. Then he tossed her over his shoulder, carried her down the stairs. She kicked her legs and struggled, but the man was too strong. He tossed her in the back of a van -- a blue van, this time.

It was freezing. The man drove the van for about 30 minutes over bumpy, twisting roads. Then the van stopped and the man took her out and carried her into another house. He dropped her onto her feet and opened a door under the stairs. Grunting from the effort, he slid a heavy trunk to one side, rolled back the cracked lino and lifted a trapdoor. There were steps leading down into the dark. She stamped her feet and yelled through her gag. She didn't want to go down there, but the man pushed her forward with his knee.

Emily stumbled down the steps and the man followed. She counted 12 steps from the trapdoor to the ground. When they reached the bottom of the stairs, he took the sticky tape from her mouth and hands. She expected him to put a manacle back on her wrist, but he didn't.

He said, "I'll be back in the morning with some friends." Then he climbed the stairs and left, closing the trapdoor with a bang. This was followed by a more distant bang that she thought must have been the front door of the house.

Emily could see nothing in the dark. She couldn't even tell if her eyes were open or closed. Even her glow-in-the-dark watch didn't work. Her arms and legs shook with fear. She knew something terrible would happen to her when the man came back with his friends. She sank to the floor and cried a little. The floor was cold and damp and there was a strong smell of mould.

After about 10 minutes she dried her eyes and began to explore the room with her hands. She found a bed against one wall, and a metal object that felt like a midget with three legs. When she explored the head she realised it was a photographer's light with a reflective dish. Feeling around the back she found an electric cable and an on/off switch. She switched it on, and the light nearly blinded her. Turning her face away, she pointed the light at a wall.

After a while her eyes began to recover from the flash. She checked the time. It was 35 minutes past midnight. She couldn't remember ever being awake that late before. She set about exploring every corner of the cellar, looking for a way out. She found a second photographer's light on a tripod and a camera mounted on a bigger tripod. There was a separate small room without a door, and inside this room, a toilet. Thank God! The only other thing she found was a spindly artificial Christmas tree, no taller than herself, standing in a corner behind the bed. Completely bare of decorations, the tree looked sad. This thought made Emily cry some more, and when it occurred to her that she might have to spend Christmas locked up in the cellar away from her parents, she lay on the bed and cried herself to sleep.

Chapter 27

It was after midnight and Jordan was exhausted, but he couldn't sleep. The idea of sleeping while Emily was at risk turned his stomach. He had a quick shower, got dressed, and walked the short distance back to The Square. The air was biting cold, the streets deserted, the street lights casting eerie shadows on the snow-covered pavements.

A phone-in centre had been set up on the ground floor to process incoming calls following Stella Carter's TV appeal. Jordan dropped in there and found 12 desks, all abandoned, each with a phone surrounded by papers. The overhead fluorescent lights were off, the only lighting in the room coming from a few desk lights. The phones were silent. Any calls received during the night would be logged by the normal telephone operators.

Jordan went through the papers on the first four desks. There were sightings of Emily from as far apart as Spain and Nigeria, offers of help from psychics and prayers from religious groups. A few were calls of support for Stella Carter. A few were hate calls from people jealous of Stella Carter's success and wealth, or malicious calls from people eager to create trouble by accusing hated neighbours.

By 1:30 am, he was at the fifth desk and starting to flag, when Garda Walescu strode into the room looking good enough to eat. Freed from its daytime constraints, her jet black hair rested on her shoulders. The subdued lighting accentuated her deep eye sockets and sharp cheekbones. She was dressed in civilian clothes, a colourful dress that followed her shapely contours.

"Oh hi, Inspector." She smiled, exposing a perfect set of teeth. "I didn't think there'd be anybody here this late."

"Couldn't sleep," said Jordan. He stared at her, marvelling at the change. Walescu in civvies was a totally different woman from the trim uniformed garda of daylight. Not for the first time it struck him how well the heavy garda uniform managed to neutralize the female form. Dressed in a standard issue uniform, even Marilyn Monroe would look like a sack of potatoes tied up with string.

She laughed. "Me too. I thought I'd go through the call records, but I see you've beaten me at it."

Jordan took a moment to respond. He had noticed small anomalies in Walescu's speech before, but still her English was exceptional.

"Beaten me to it," he said.

"Oh sorry, Inspector, my English is not perfect yet."

He said, "How did a Romanian girl become an Irish police officer?"

She shrugged. "My father has a sheep farm. I have two brothers. There was nothing for me there. I studied English and came to Ireland as soon as I could. I like it here."

She pulled a chair from one of the other desks and perched on it. As she crossed her legs, Jordan got an eyeful, well above the knee.

"Really, your English is very good," he said. "How long have you been a garda?"

"A year. And I have been working with Inspector Flood for six months."

"You like working with Inspector Flood?"

She smiled, and her face lit up. "Oh yes, the job makes him angry some times, but he always treats me with respect. He gives me interesting jobs to do. Nothing is ever boring in the Domestic Violence and Sexual Abuse Unit."

"How did you get posted to the DV Unit? I would have thought it might be a difficult environment…" Walescu's panic attack at the orphanage was a strong indicator that she was in the wrong section, if not the wrong job altogether.

"For a woman, you mean, Inspector?" She leaned forward. With a rush, Jordan was struck by her sexuality. In any other situation he would have thought she was flirting with him. "Inspector Flood picked me. Some of the images I see are difficult to look at, and some of the people we have to deal with are unpleasant, but, as Inspector Flood says, somebody has to do it."

"How did Liam Flood pick you? Did you know him before you joined the force?"

"We were friends, yes."

Jordan's phone beeped with an incoming text from Eddie Duignan in the Garda Technical Bureau. Jordan excused himself and rang the number.

"Ben," Duignan shouted down the phone. "We have a result." The scientist was having difficulty suppressing his excitement. "We have two identical strands of hair. One I took from Emily's hairbrush, the other we found in the back of the van."

"O'Reilly's van? You're sure?" said Jordan.

"I'd stake my reputation on it, Ben. Emily Carter was in that van."

"Who else knows?" said Jordan.

"Just Superintendent Lassiter. I assumed he would spread the word."

No doubt about it, thought Jordan.

He terminated the call and gave Walescu the good news. She leapt from her chair with excitement and ran to make all the necessary phone calls. The Special Detective Unit would be informed, O'Reilly's name would be bumped to the top of the most wanted list and his photograph circulated to every Garda station in the country within minutes.

Jordan called Flood. Flood picked up straight away and when Jordan gave him the news he gave a whoop of delight. "I knew it! O'Reilly has her."

"Now all we have to do is find O'Reilly," said Jordan. "Is there any known connection between O'Reilly and the IRA or O'Reilly and Crowe?"

"None. As far as I know O'Reilly has never shown the slightest interest in politics."

Chapter 28

As Jordan drove west the clock on his dashboard read 2:01 am. A fresh sprinkling of snow began to fall. A stray thought came to the surface of his mind. PULSE, the Garda computer system, had said that the two suspects, Budgie Bolger and Adam O'Reilly were associates, but there was nothing on O'Reilly's permanent file to back that up. How were the two men connected?

When he arrived at O'Reilly's house, he found an Armed Response Unit, led by Superintendent Harry Tierney, waiting for him: a black transport van filled with men dressed in black fatigues, B-P vests and armed with Uzi submachine guns. Flood was there too, in his car.

"There's no need for guns, Harry," Jordan told Tierney. "Tell your men to stay where they are."

"I have my orders," said Tierney. "O'Reilly could be armed. We have to protect the child."

"For God's sake, keep the men back. Let me and Flood go in first -- alone. We'll call if we need you."

Tierney had no choice but to agree. He ordered his men into defensive positions at the front and back of the house. It was Jordan's case. If Tierney acted against Jordan's wishes and anything went wrong, he would have to bear the full consequences.

Jordan and Flood hammered on the door. When no one answered they let themselves in through the back door as they had before. The house was deserted. Jordan put on a pair of latex gloves and handed a second pair to Flood.

"We should get a search warrant," said Flood. "If we find anything incriminating it'll be inadmissible."

Jordan gave Flood a look that said: you cannot be serious. Flood shrugged and snapped on the gloves. Jordan opened a front window and signalled all-clear to Harry Tierney. Tierney entered the house and conducted his own search before ordering his squad into their transport and leaving the scene.

Flood powered up O'Reilly's computer. He pressed the eject

button on the CD reader and a CD slid out. Flood bagged it and slipped it into his pocket.

Jordan said, "You can switch the computer off. It's password-protected."

They went through the house room by room collecting paperwork. There were utility bills, bank statements, old pamphlets from colleges, travel agents, deceased politicians…

"This is all shit," Flood called from upstairs. "We don't need any of this stuff."

"Take everything," Jordan replied.

Moving his weight over the living room carpet, a floorboard creaked. Jordan lifted a corner of the carpet to reveal a loose floorboard. Prising the floorboard up, he slid a hand in and pulled out a VHS cassette. He bagged it, felt around for more and found nothing.

30 minutes later they loaded O'Reilly's computer, the VHS cassette, and a sack full of papers into the boot of Jordan's car. It was 3 am, exactly 12 hours since the abduction.

Jordan ordered a testy Flood home to get some sleep. Jordan intended to do the same himself, but the news from the Technical Bureau was like a shot of raw adrenalin. He went directly to Harcourt Square, hauled the sack of papers into the lift and got out on the third floor. The Incident Room was deserted. He emptied the sack onto his desk. The VHS cassette fell out and slid to the floor. He put it into the video player and pressed 'play'.

The movie started without preamble. It featured two girls, maybe nine and eleven years old, and two masked men, one tall. The action started within a minute. There was no pretence at setting a scene; the men simply took it in turns with the children on a bed. As he watched Jordan gripped the arms of the chair, and tried to remain objective, to find clues to the location. The scene was well-lit. Apart from the bed and a miserable-looking artificial Christmas tree standing in the corner, the room was featureless. Jordan's scalp crawled; he reached for the eject button, but hesitated when the scene changed. One of the men slapped the older girl across the face. He struck her again with a closed fist. The second girl was no longer in the frame, although Jordan could hear her screaming. He watched with increasing horror as the beating became more and more severe.

With a trembling hand, he switched it off. He knew how it would end. His blood boiled, his hands became fists. With no outlet for his rage, he struggled for calm and a feeling of numbness spread over his mind. He closed his eyes. Graphic images from what he had seen flashed behind his eyelids. His head spun and his hands continued to shake. In his 20 years on the force he couldn't count the number of ways he'd seen people abuse others. He'd seen sadistic violence and death, fatal gunshot wounds, stabbings, dismembered bodies; he'd witnessed his own daughter lose her soul to heroin; but what he'd just seen was far worse.

Gangland killings were motivated by greed, interfamily feuds by revenge, racist attacks had their roots in ignorance and hatred, and many domestic killers were driven by lust. In his experience all murders could be explained by cause and effect. But Jordan could find no chain of reasoning -- however warped -- that would lead to the cold-blooded killing of two children. He was not a religious man, but he had always known that 'evil' was more than an abstract concept. It stalked the world, manifesting itself in countless forms. The men who made that movie were truly evil, inhuman monsters.

And he would move mountains to find them.

A great weariness swept over him. He needed a drink. Badly. He licked his dry lips and put the thought out of his mind. Gathering his shattered mental resources, he swore he'd see those men behind bars.

That was when it came to him with absolute certainty that this would be his last case on the force.

Chapter 29

He bagged the video cassette and sent it and O'Reilly's computer to the Garda Technical Bureau by courier, enclosing a warning note addressed to Eddie Duignan, the lab technician, about the contents of the cassette. Then he went through O'Reilly's papers. Almost immediately he came across a brown envelope containing O'Reilly's bank statements going back ten years. He leafed through them quickly and noted regular injections of cash amounting to €120,000 each year. Jordan wondered if these could be IRA funds.

He rang his old IRA contact, Packie. Packie picked up on the third attempt. "This better be good." He coughed.

"Sorry to wake you, Packie. I need to ask you a question."

"Ben, is that you? What the hell time is it?"

"Half past three," said Jordan. "What can you tell me about Adam O'Reilly?"

"Never heard of him. What's he done?"

"Take your time. Think carefully, Packie. It's important. I need to know if Adam O'Reilly was ever connected to the IRA or any republican organisation."

Packie took a moment to gather his thoughts.

"Where's he from, North or South?"

"South. He's a Dubliner."

"How old is he?"

"He was born in 1950. Fifty-four give or take."

"There was an O'Reilly in the Real IRA, Derry command, but his name wasn't Adam. Desmond, Derek. Dermot! Yes, that was it, Dermot O'Reilly. But he would've been a lot older. No, I'm sure I've never come across an Adam O'Reilly."

"How about Tom Dwyer?"

Packie's slight hesitation told Jordan all he needed to know. Stella Carter's ex-employee was a member of one or other of the republican movements. "Don't know that name either."

"Thanks, Packie. Any word on this Joint Command?"

Packie coughed into the phone again before answering. "Give us a chance, Ben. Don't you ever sleep?"

#

At 5 am the early shift found him slumped over his desk, sleeping. He drove home to get cleaned up. It was snowing heavily now, the streets of the city covered in four inches of the stuff -- more than enough to cause traffic panic in Dublin, where snow is as rare an occurrence as a dry day. The dawn chorus was in full swing. Jordan thought the birds sounded louder than usual, as if excited by the rare sight of their world painted white.

By 5:30 he'd had a shower, two slices of dry bread and a lukewarm cup of coffee. His radio was on, its early morning nonsense doing a poor job of drowning out the sights and sounds of the snuff movie that refused to leave him.

His phone rang. It was Kate. The first time she'd rung him since the split.

"Good morning, Kate," he said. "It's early, even for you."

"You have the divorce papers." He hardly recognized her voice. It was as if she'd scrubbed all the humanity from it.

"I wanted to talk to you--"

"There's nothing to talk about. Just sign the papers."

"I've been incredibly busy, searching for Emily Carter," he said.

"We're all busy. It won't take you two minutes to sign."

"We need to discuss this, Kate. It's a pretty big step."

"There's nothing to discuss. I've given it a lot of thought, and it's what I want."

"Have you thought about what I want?" said Ben. "We should meet and talk about it."

"There's no point, Ben. I can't live with you as long as you're doing that job."

She hung up.

He shivered his way to the car. Jesus, the poor child must be freezing -- if she's still alive. He thought about the video he'd seen. Something was nagging at him, something on the tape had stirred a memory. An SUV like Kate's cut across in front of him, horn blaring. He'd run a red light. Then he started to re-run the conversation with Kate. Once upon a time they had been as close as two people could be. They had an understanding that transcended speech, a way of reflecting each other like mirrors. He could pick her out from the back of her head in a crowd of 10 thousand, and he could tell her mood from the way she tilted her face, from the merest gesture or flicker of an eyelid. She knew him just as well. When he played his piano, the strings told her everything she needed to know about his innermost feelings.

He had always thought that they were a perfect couple. Well, not perfect -- their jobs prevented that -- but they did seem ideally suited. That Kate could contemplate divorce was unconscionable, and yet there was no denying those papers or her coldness on the phone. Nothing could shake his fundamental belief in the family unit -- in their family unit. Any other arrangement would be crazy. He loved Kate. He loved Lucy. Ben had been brought up by his mother and her father, both now dead. When push came to shove, Kate and Lucy were the only two people left in his life.

He parked the car and trudged into The Square, his spirits as dark and cold as the morning.

Chapter 30

By 6 am Jordan was standing by the window of the Incident Room. Outside was the very picture of Christmas. The snow was falling thick and heavy. He could barely see the festive lights down the centre of Harcourt Street or the buildings across the street. The traffic was at a standstill. Emily was out there somewhere. Jordan couldn't shake the feeling that he'd been set up. Lassiter hated his guts and nothing would please the super more than to see Jordan fail. Finding one schoolgirl in a city the size of Dublin was never going to be easy, but now that everything was covered in snow it seemed impossible.

Flood sat opposite Jordan's desk, his hands wrapped around a polystyrene cup. He looked as bad as Jordan felt.

"Rough night?" said Jordan.

Flood suppressed a yawn. "I spent the last few hours going through the images on that CD. I'm not sure I'll ever fully recover from the experience."

"Anything there to help find Emily?"

"Not a lot. It's going to take years to identify all the children, and we'll need help from Europol. All of these kids will be non-nationals smuggled into the country." Flood took a slug from his cup and grimaced.

"How can you be sure the images were taken in Ireland?"

"I recognize the camera's properties, and we've seen the room before."

"But you don't know where it is?" said Jordan.

"No."

"How many children are we talking about?"

"Twelve in total, all ages from six up to about ten."

Jordan took a couple of moments to absorb the horror implied by this information. "Any chance of identifying the adults?"

Flood waved a hand dismissively. "Not a hope. They're all wearing masks."

"What about Emily?"

"She wasn't featured, thank God. The most recent images were taken about a month ago."

"Let me take a look," said Jordan, grimly.

Flood put the CD in Jordan's computer CD player. The directory listed 50 images with innocuous names 'PRB001 to PRB050'. Gingerly, Jordan opened one of the files at random. The image that confronted him was a horrific still picture of a child and an adult. The scene was well-lit, and Jordan immediately recognized the bed, and the miserable artificial Christmas tree that he'd seen in the snuff movie. Fresh images from the movie flashed into his mind. His brain began to freeze again. A single bead of sweat broke out on his forehead and slid down his nose.

He ejected the CD and handed it back to Flood.

When Garda Walescu arrived Jordan said, "I'd like you to help me take a look through this lot," indicating the stack of papers on his desk from the raid on O'Reilly's house. "A fresh set of eyes might turn something up."

Walescu grabbed a chair and sat beside Jordan at his desk. "What are we looking for?"

Jordan said, "Anything that might tell us where O'Reilly could be."

"And anything linking him to the IRA," said Flood.

The phone on Jordan's desk rang and Walescu picked it up. After a short conversation she replaced the phone. "That was Superintendent Lassiter. He wants you in his office, Inspector Jordan, sir."

Flood tossed his empty cup into a wastebasket with a mumbled obscenity and went off to his own office.

Jordan stood up and put his jacket on. "Bag everything as you go, Mary. And see if you can find the connection between O'Reilly and Bolger."

He took the lift to the sixth floor.

Superintendent Lassiter had a serene expression on his face. He invited Jordan into his office with a regal wave.

"You wanted to see me," Jordan said, taking the chair nearest the door.

"Yes, Inspector. How's the search going?"

"We have made some headway."

"The lab report." Lassiter steepled his fingers.

"Yes. We have confirmation that Emily was abducted in Adam O'Reilly's van."

"Good. And have you apprehended O'Reilly yet?"

"Not yet."

"You received the lab report when?"

"At about two o'clock this morning."

Lassiter made a show of checking his watch. "A little over four hours ago."

"He seems to have gone to ground."

"I see. Have you established a connection between O'Reilly and the IRA?"

"No. There doesn't seem to be one."

Lassiter interlocked his fingers as if in prayer. "But surely there must be one. If O'Reilly's van was used and the IRA have the child, it follows that O'Reilly must be a member of the IRA grouping."

"I don't think so," said Jordan. He had the feeling that Lassiter hadn't come to the real point of the interview. "The IRA Joint Command hasn't provided any proof that they have Emily. It's highly probable that their intervention is an opportunistic attempt to extort funds."

"You don't think they have the child?"

"I can't be sure, but if they don't produce any proof the next time they call, we won't be paying them any money."

"How do the parents feel about that?"

"I couldn't say. I will try to persuade them not to part with the money unless the caller provides proof."

Lassiter paused. He placed his hands on the arms of his chair and leaned forward.

"I hear you interviewed a suspect last night."

Here we go.

"Peter Green. He gave us information that led indirectly to O'Reilly."

"I have had a disturbing report about the interrogation."

"Oh?"

"Green has made a complaint that he was mistreated during his interrogation by you and Inspector Flood."

"An official complaint?"

"Not official, not so far, but we still have to take it seriously. He says he was beaten, and he claims to have health issues."

"I take full responsibility for what happened," said Jordan.

"Damn right, you do," said Lassiter, his eyes blazing. "This is your investigation. Whatever happens on your watch is entirely your responsibility."

#

On his way back to his office, Jordan thought about the divorce papers awaiting his signature back at the house. Signing the papers seemed the path of least resistance, but his heart rebelled against the idea. He resolved to try to talk Kate out of it. If she knew he'd already resigned... If there was any spark left...

He paused on the staircase and rang her mobile phone.

A man's voice answered: "Doctor Kate Jordan's phone." An Irish accent but with an English twist.

"Who's this?" said Jordan.

"Who wants to know?"

"Ben Jordan, Kate's husband."

"Feck off," said the man, and he broke the connection.

Chapter 31

Emily awoke in darkness. It took a moment or two to remember what had happened and where she was. She had left the studio light on, but it had failed while she slept, or else there had been a power failure.

She got to her feet shakily and took a few steps toward the studio light. She tried the on/off switch, but it was dead. She groped around and found another light that toppled over with a crash. She checked that it was plugged into a wall socket before trying the on/off switch. Nothing. She searched around some more and found the bigger tripod with the camera mounted on top.

Shivering with the cold, she found the toilet and used it.

Then she groped her way to the bottom step and climbed, counting the 12 steps to the top. She tried the trapdoor. It moved a tiny bit, but it was really heavy. She shouted. "Help! Help me. Anybody?"

She tried the door again. She made fists and pounded on it. She screamed. When she'd used up all her screams, she felt her way down to the bottom of the stairs and along the wall to one of the tripod lights. She unplugged it and, hugging it to herself, stepped gingerly across the floor, and navigated the steps again. Using all her strength she managed to open the door wide enough to slide one leg of the tripod into the crack. She could see a tiny light through the crack. She went down to the bottom again and picked up the second light as well as the tall tripod with the camera. She forced one leg of the second light into the gap, and then she used a leg of the large tripod to prise the door open some more. Now she could put her hand through the gap. She could feel the jagged edge of the linoleum. She began to get excited. She was making progress!

With another supreme effort, she jammed all three legs of one of the studio lights into the gap. Then she was able to prise open the door, remove the first tripod and force all three of its legs in as well. The camera fell off its tripod and she hurled it down the steps. Next, she jammed the three legs of the camera tripod into the gap. This allowed her to wedge it open with the two lights by turning them on their sides. This was the hardest part. She had to use her back to hold the door open, and several times she nearly lost all that she'd gained. But she managed it. The door was open just wide enough to allow her to squeeze her head through. She swallowed some dust from the lino, but she kept going. She was half way out when one of the dishes wobbled, then slipped sideways and fell. The weight of the door began to crush the second dish, and the opening narrowed, squashing her hips. Close to panic, she hauled herself out and swung her legs clear just as the second dish collapsed under the weight of the door. The second tripod disappeared from sight, following its companion down into the cellar with a muffled clatter. She kicked the camera tripod inward and the trapdoor snapped shut, raising a cloud of dust.

Emily was elated. She had taken her first steps toward freedom! She stood in the hallway and took a moment to brush the dust from her face and clothes and to get her breath. Heading toward the stairs, she tripped over something and bent down to see what it was. Her coat. She was happy to find it and she slipped it on.

When she looked out through the window she got a shock. Snow was falling, and everything was cloaked in a thick white layer. It was 6 am, Sunday morning. There was light in the sky, but the sun had not yet risen. The birds were singing their heads off. They sounded happy. She envied them. They were free; she was locked up in a strange house at the mercy of horrible evil men.

She explored the building, visiting every room, hoping to find a phone, terrified of meeting one of the men. Before entering each room, she called out, "Hello?" and held her breath. If anyone had answered she would have died of a heart attack. No one did. The building was huge -- much bigger than her school. Counting the dark cellar and its toilet, there were 29 rooms in four storeys, all empty, all smelling of damp, dust, and mould.

The view through the upstairs rear windows was of an untidy garden backing onto trees, and she could just make out three dogs prowling about outside.

She went downstairs again and opened a window at the back of the building. Two of the dogs appeared immediately and snarled at her, baring their teeth.

She thought about what she might do and quickly made up her mind. The one thing she wasn't going to do was wait around for the man to come back with his friends.

She slid the window open wider and put her head out. Both dogs showed their fangs under quivering upper lips.

Emily held out a hand to the dogs and said, "Here boys. Nice doggies."

One dog barked. Both dogs snarled.

"Now don't be nasty, be nice," she said.

The dogs hesitated for a moment before they both took a step forward, snarling. Emily closed the window. She was at a loss what to do next. Then she heard a car engine at the front. The dogs ran around to the front of the house to investigate. Seizing her chance, she opened the window, climbed out, and made a dash down the garden.

By the time she reached the wall at the end of the garden, she was covered in wet sticky snow, her shoes were wet through and her feet stung from the cold. A single dog appeared and snarled at her heels. Emily frowned at the dog with her hands on her hips.

"By nice," she said. "Sit!"

The dog sat back on his haunches.

"Good dog," said Emily, and she began to climb the wall.

All three dogs watched as she scaled the ivy-clad wall and dropped over the other side. As soon as she was out of sight they all began to bark.

"Quiet!" Emily shouted, and the dogs stopped barking.

Chapter 32

Under its white blanket the woodland looked magical and dark, the trees growing close together, their branches so intertwined and tangled, that little of the snow had penetrated to the ground. As she walked toward the trees the snow continued to fall, thicker than ever, filling her footprints. Inside the wood she found a narrow path and followed it.

It was eerily quiet; there were no bird sounds in the wood. Deeper into the wood the going got tougher. The path became narrower and narrower, until it disappeared altogether. Faced with tightly packed trees on all sides, she chose the most likely way forward, pushing through the tangled branches and undergrowth, stumbling on exposed roots, her wet shoes making her slip at almost every step. And then the trees were too densely packed to allow her to go forward.

She stopped, leant against a tree trunk and tried to work out what she should do next. She couldn't go back. She couldn't stay where she was; her feet were too wet, too cold and the men would be coming for her. She had to keep moving, but she wasn't sure which way to go. Then she heard the sound of a car engine up ahead, quite close by. She set out toward the sound.

The first few yards were the hardest, but then she came to a clearing and found the path again. The path took her deeper into the undergrowth, twisting and turning so much that she was no longer sure she was moving away from the house, that the path wasn't leading her right back where she started. She was beginning to think she'd never find her way out of the wood, when the path forked. She chose to go left. Then she came to a crossroads. She now had three choices, left, right or straight on. She chose straight on. Soon, the trees thinned and she came out of the wood onto a country road flanked on both sides by ditches and hedges.

She listened, but heard no cars.

There was no traffic on the road, only the tyre marks from just one car, almost completely covered by fresh snow. She got to the centre of the road and followed it to the left. After a short distance she spotted a lone farmhouse on a hill, and her heart soared. She could get help here. She would soon be home and safe with her mammy and her daddy.

The hill was difficult to climb, the snow deep and fresh, but she was encouraged by the smell of a turf fire and the sight of smoke rising from the farmhouse chimney. By the time she arrived at the farmhouse door she was exhausted. She took a moment to take a few deep breaths before banging on the door.

The door was opened by a grey-haired woman with an old sheepdog by her side.

"Merciful heaven," said the woman. "Where did you spring from, child? Come inside. You must be frozen solid."

Inside the farmhouse an elderly man sat by a turf fire watching TV.

Emily's coat was wet through and covered in snow. Her shoes were ruined, her fingers, her legs and her feet close to frostbite. The woman shook the snow off Emily's coat and hung it on a clotheshorse near the fire; her shoes and socks she propped on the hearth to dry.

"You sit there and warm up, and I'll get you a cup of something," the woman said. Emily sat in an armchair on the other side of the fire from the man. The woman lifted a rug off the couch and snuggled it around her, and the sheepdog lay down at Emily's feet.

The old man asked her name and where she came from. Emily told him. Then she told him the whole story -- about the man who had picked her up and tied her with sticky tape and the other man who'd fed her.

Emily heard the old woman in the kitchen making clicking sounds in her mouth.

"They didn't do anything to you?" said the old farmer.

Emily wasn't sure how to answer this question. Perhaps the old man was deaf and hadn't heard her story.

"Leave her be," said the woman from the kitchen. "Poor mite, she must be exhausted. We need to dry her clothes and let her get some rest."

"I'd like to call my daddy, to tell him I'm okay," said Emily.

"Of course you would, child. Joe, show Emily where the phone is."

The man made no move to get up. Instead, he poked at the fire and said, "The phone's broke, remember."

The woman paused before replying, "Oh yes, I forgot. I'm sorry, dear, we can't call your parents. But we can make a call from a neighbour's house." She handed Emily a cup and a plate of scones before shuffling off and returning with a pen and paper. "Write down the number, a leanbh, and Joe can call them."

Emily wrote the number and gave it to the woman. Then she wrapped her icy fingers around the mug of hot cocoa, and gobbled down the whole plate of currant scones dripping with salty butter.

They sat by the fire for the best part of an hour, warmth gradually returning to Emily's fingers and toes. The farmer made no move to visit the neighbours and make the call, and nobody mentioned it again. Emily wondered if the old couple had forgotten, or maybe the neighbours were miles away across the fields and they had to wait for the snow to stop.

Emily was tired and she said so. It had been really late when she slept in the cellar, and she'd woken early. The woman showed her into a bedroom. "This used to be our son's room before he left home," she said.

Emily lay down on the bed.

The woman said, "That's it, you get some sleep. You'll feel a lot better when you wake up again."

Emily closed her eyes.

Chapter 33

Jordan reached the Incident Room slightly out of breath. Sergeant Payne had arrived and Jordan filled him in on the news from the Garda Technical Bureau. They agreed a programme of work for the day for the team. The phones would be manned and all relevant phone records would be checked.

Payne counted the names on his fingers: "O'Reilly, Frank Hughes the site foreman, Peter Green, and Billy Bolger."

"And Dinny Kenny," Walescu added.

"Yes, check them all," said Jordan. "And check all their financial records too, while you're at it."

Garda Walescu presented Jordan with a fresh cup of coffee. She handed him two pieces of paper. One was a single-page summary of O'Reilly's criminal record, the other was Billy Bolger's.

"What am I looking at?" said Jordan. The coffee was strong and hot.

"You see nothing unusual?" Walescu smiled. Jordan frowned at her. He was too weary for mind games. "Take a look at the dates of birth, sir."

Jordan's heart skipped a beat. O'Reilly and Bolger were both born on the same day: February 4, 1950. Could that be a coincidence? The same calendar day, maybe, but the same day in the same year?

Walescu said, "I wondered, could Bolger and O'Reilly be the same person? That would explain why we haven't been able to find O'Reilly."

Jordan took another look at the two records. The photographs were completely different, although photographs can he altered or substituted. Likewise the fingerprints.

"I don't think so," said the sergeant. "O'Reilly's nearly six foot tall; Bolger's only five foot six inches."

Jordan rang Flood and told him what Walescu had discovered.

"That's easily explained," said Flood. "We know they are associates. My guess is that they were both brought up in St Benedict's orphanage."

"I don't follow," said Jordan.

"Whenever children arrived at the orphanage without any records, the staff would give them notional birth dates."

Jordan said, "But the same birth date?"

"You can take it that both boys were admitted on the same day, probably that same calendar day, February fourth."

"So where does that get us?"

"Nowhere, really. We know they are associates. We know they're both into child abuse. Now we know where they first met."

After the call Jordan said to Walescu, "Nice work, Mary, but Inspector Flood has a simple explanation." He looked at his watch. "I need to get back to Stepaside to take the IRA phone call at seven."

"You don't believe the IRA have Emily, do you, sir?"

"No, I don't."

"Me too," she said.

"What about me, sir?" said Walescu. "Anything special you'd like me to do?"

Jordan replied, "Help the sergeant. And stay close to the phone. I may need you."

"I feel so worried about Emily, in the hands of those -- those men. We really need to find her quickly. If I could take her place I would. No child should be put through what... what those evil men do."

Walescu looked on the verge of tears. Jordan put that down to lack of sleep.

"Don't upset yourself, Mary," he said. "I'm sure we will find her." He wasn't as confident as he sounded.

Chapter 34

The house looked like a Siberian dacha. Thick snow covered the roof and the land all around it as well as Stella Carter's VW Golf and the unmarked Garda car in the driveway. Quigley's Lexus was missing. It had exited the premises sometime during the night, leaving ghostly tyre tracks in the snow. The snow was still falling.

Emily's grey-faced mother met Jordan at the door. He held out a hand to her but she ignored it. He followed her to a living room where Garda David Irwin was attending the telephone. Stella Carter sat on one end of a settee and Jordan took the other end of the three-seater.

He caught Irwin's eye. Irwin said, "Nothing so far, sir."

It was 6:45 am.

"You have the money, Ms Carter?" said Jordan.

She produced a blue sports bag. Jordan opened it.

"How much is here?" he said.

"Close to €400,000. It's all we could manage in the time." Her face showed the effects of extreme anxiety, too little sleep, and too much wine. She looked ten years older than she had the day before.

"It'll have to do," said Jordan. "When the call comes Garda Irwin will take it."

Jordan was surprised that Shane Quigley wasn't there to receive the expected call from the IRA Joint Command. "Where's Emily's father?" he said.

Stella instantly established eye contact. "Shane left the house last night at about midnight. I haven't seen him since, and he's not answering his phone."

"Did he say anything before he left? Did he say where he was going?"

"He said he wasn't going to sit around waiting for... waiting for something to happen. He has some police training, you know, from when he lived in New York." Stella licked her lips. "Have the searches produced anything? What about our TV appeal?"

"We are following a definite line of enquiry," said Jordan, "Does the name Adam O'Reilly mean anything to you?"

"No. Should I know him? Who is he?"

"He may be connected," said Jordan, vaguely.

Stella picked through a pile of newspapers on a coffee table. She handed The Irish Independent to Jordan. "This paper claims that Emily's disappearance may be the work of organised criminal gangs. It says these gangs traffic children into Ireland." Before Jordan could respond, she handed him The Daily Bulletin. The lead article, under the by-line Declan Fairweather, covered the dissident republican angle. Stella turned to an inside page. "There's a story here about someone called Richardson -- a known paedophile --" Her voice broke.

Jordan said, "You don't want to pay any attention to the newspapers, Ms Carter. They don't have any real information -- and Emily's disappearance is the biggest story they've had all year."

"So there's nothing to any of these stories?"

"Probably not," said Jordan. "We've spoken to Richardson. He's not a suspect. And these traffickers bring children into the country from overseas for the Irish sex industry, not the other way around."

"That's horrible," she said. "What's being done about it?"

"We have a team working on it," said Jordan.

After a pause, the businesswoman said, "Tell me about this Adam O'Reilly."

"He's a suspect," said Jordan.

"A strong suspect?"

"You could say that, yes."

Stella straightened her back. It was if a light was switched on behind her eyes.

"You have this man in custody?"

"We're looking for him."

The light faded. She said, "Shane told me he was drafted onto the investigation. Is that true?"

"Well, no. We agreed to keep him informed."

"When did you last see him?"

"I haven't seen him, not since we all met here last night. He offered to help with the investigation."

"That's just like him. He's probably out there somewhere 'investigating'."

"Meaning what?"

"Throwing his weight around, threatening people, making things worse." Then, in a faltering voice, she said, "If you see him,

Inspector, tell him to come home. Tell him to contact me. I'm not sure I can do this without him."

Jordan couldn't imagine what the American might be up to. So far outside the NYPD catchment area, and in unfamiliar territory, he could be causing untold damage to the actual search.

On the stroke of 7 am the telephone rang. Stella had been prowling about the room like a caged tiger. When the phone rang she gave a tiny squeal. Irwin checked that his recorder and loudspeaker were switched on before picking it up.

"Listen carefully." An electronically distorted voice. "You must take the money to the Phoenix Park and drop it in the litter bin at the Ashtown Gate at exactly 10 o'clock today. The child will be returned when we have the money and Robert Emmet Crowe has been released. Do you understand?"

"I'd like to speak to Emily," Garda Irwin said.

"Who is this? Put the American on."

"Mr Quigley is not available," said Irwin. "I can speak on his behalf."

"Don't play games with us. Put the American on the line."

"He's not here. You'll have to deal with me. The family has not been able to raise all the money."

A pause. "How much have they got?"

"Four hundred thousand."

The caller paused again. "Well they have three hours to find the rest."

"They can't raise any more," said Irwin. Beads of sweat had appeared on his brow.

"Don't give me that. They're rich."

"All their money is tied up in their businesses."

The caller hesitated for three beats. "Well in that case they won't see their daughter again alive. Make sure they drop off the full million and that Robert Emmet Crowe is released. Otherwise the deal is off."

Stella stuffed a fist in her mouth.

Jordan took the phone from Irwin. "Let me speak to Emily."

"Who's this?"

"Detective Inspector Ben Jordan. Put Emily on."

A short pause. "Not going to happen. She's not here."

"How do I know you have her?"

"You'll just have to take my word for it."

Jordan said, "We'll have to hear Emily's voice before the exchange. If you can't put Emily on the phone we won't part with a red cent."

After another short pause, the voice said, "If Stella Carter wants her daughter back in one piece you'll play by my rules, copper." The caller disconnected.

Red in the face, Stella shouted at Jordan, "What was that? Is that your idea of negotiation?"

"Calm yourself, Ms Carter," said Jordan. "We have to get proof that these people have Emily before any money changes hands."

"You're crazy!" screamed Stella. "We must do whatever they say. I want my little girl back."

Garda Irwin said, "Inspector Jordan is right, Ma'am. We need positive proof, and then the exchange will have to be handled very carefully. We don't want to hand over the money until we're sure that Emily will be released."

Stella pulled a mobile phone from her bag and selected a number. When the call was answered she introduced herself and asked for Superintendent Lassiter. "Well ask the superintendent to call me as soon as he gets in. He has my number." She swept out of the room.

Garda Irwin looked like a man who'd lost a shilling and found sixpence.

"Stick by the phone," said Jordan. "If they have Emily they will ring back. If they do, or anything else happens let me know immediately."

He rang Flood and told him that Quigley had gone missing.

"I'll get the team to check the flights to the USA," said Flood.

"You don't really think Quigley abducted his own daughter?"

"It follows the classic pattern of parental abductions," Flood said. "It's still a long shot, but we have to check."

Chapter 35

Frank Hughes tied the dogs to their constraint bar as Dinny Kenny opened the front door. Then both men stepped into the building.

"You alerted the others?" said Kenny.

"I called them both. They should be here within the hour."

"Right, secure the girl and get everything set up. We'll start as soon as they get here. We'll need to do this quickly if she's to leave on the noon sailing."

Hughes grunted as he lifted the trapdoor under the stairs. It was made from fibreboard and bloody heavy. He let it fall with a crash against the wall. Four steps down into the cellar, he reached for the light switch.

"Shit! The power's out, boss."

"Check the fuse box," said Kenny. "I'll wait here."

Hughes hurried off to the kitchen area. Kenny peered down into the cellar.

"Hello down there," he called out. "Em-mily. Where are you, sweetheart?"

He laughed when there was no response. "Cat got your tongue, has it?"

The cellar light came on, and Kenny descended the steps. Hughes followed him down.

"Coo-ee, Emil-ly. Where are you?" Kenny sang out. He reached the bottom of the stairs and said, "Come out, come out wherever you are." His foot caught one of the studio lights and he stumbled. "Fuck! This light's in bits. What's the little brat been up to?"

Kenny looked around the room. Both studio lights were smashed and the camera was missing from its tripod. The girl wasn't anywhere in the cellar.

"She's not here, boss," said Hughes.

Kenny picked up the pieces of the broken camera. "The little bitch..."

Hughes said, "She must have got out."

Kenny said, "How the fuck did she manage that? Didn't I tell you to cover the trapdoor? Never mind. Go find her. She must be somewhere in the building."

They climbed out of the cellar and Hughes went off to search the building. Kenny lit a cigar and stood at one of the front windows looking into the garden. The dogs were there, barely visible in the snow. There was something strange about them. These three looked nothing like the vicious guard dogs he had paid for. Where was the snarling aggression, the mindless lupine violence? Fierce alert glares had been replaced by droopy soporific eyes. He had paid for dogs with enough attitude to tear a full grown stag limb from limb; these guys looked as if they'd lick Bambi to death.

The site manager reappeared. "Christ, I'm screwed," he said. "She's definitely gone."

"Gone? Gone where? How could she be gone?"

"Listen, boss, I need to disappear fast. The cops'll hang me out to dry if they catch me."

"Just stay calm, Frank. She must be in the building. Look again. She's hiding somewhere."

Frank Hughes's face reddened. "I've looked everywhere. She's not here, boss."

"Don't panic. Everything will be fine. We just have to find her."

"If she reaches safety, Dinny, I'm a goner. She can identify me."

"Search the grounds," said Kenny. "Maybe the dogs ate her. They sure look well fed."

Hughes searched the grounds, and reported back with a forlorn shake of his head. "I'm toast."

"What did I just say?"

"Yeah, but I'm the one in the headlights, boss, O'Reilly too. She's never seen you."

Kenny glared at him. "O'Reilly has more important things to worry about. If we don't find her in time to ship her out on that ferry we're all screwed. The Russian will have our balls for kebabs." Kenny checked his watch. "We have four hours. Ring me when you find her. I'll pick up a new camera and some studio lights and meet you back here."

Chapter 36

Jordan left Stepaside and returned to The Square. He checked the call centre. A dozen reported sightings of Emily were being investigated in various far-flung corners of the country, none of which sounded remotely promising.

He took the lift to Flood's office and they reviewed the case together. Neither man could think of an obvious next step. The investigation had hit a brick wall.

"We need to locate O'Reilly. Where the fuck could he be hiding?" said Jordan, pacing up and down in front of Flood's desk.

Flood said, "I still have one or two names of my list."

"List? What list?"

"Sex offenders with vans, remember? We could interview the rest of them."

"You do that." Jordan waved an arm. "Let me know if anything turns up."

Flood left. Jordan continued to pace. After a few minutes he hurried to the Incident Room and picked up a copy of the Daily Bulletin. The story that Stella Carter had mentioned was about paedophiles living in anonymity amongst the general population. It showed a grainy photograph of Richardson. The bar across his eyes did little to disguise his identity and the picture was captioned with his full name. The gist of the article was that people with sexual offence convictions of any kind should be clearly identified to help protect society from their predatory activities. Jordan dropped the paper, threw on his coat, and went in search of his car.

The two officers at O'Reilly's house had pulled the shortest of short straws, watching over an empty house in a freezing squad car. They had nothing to report.

He let himself in through the back door for the third time and began to search again. He started with the loose floorboard, but found nothing under there. In the kitchen he opened all the cupboards, emptying and checking containers of coffee, tea, pasta, running his fingers through the contents. He searched the living room again, but found nothing. Everything was exactly as they had left it. He climbed the stairs and checked the three bedrooms. He looked under the mattresses and checked each of the bedroom wardrobes. Nothing, nothing and nothing.

He checked the bathroom. Nothing there either.

He went back to the living room, sat in an armchair and lit a cigarette. He was sure he must have missed something. Surveying the room once more his eyes fell on the computer monitor, the keyboard, the printer and the dust patch left behind by the computer.

He called the Garda Technical Bureau and spoke to Eddie Duignan. "Any news about O'Reilly's computer?"

"We've cracked the password. The hard disk is full of porn, mostly child porn."

"Anything else?"

"There are lots of files that look like consignment notes for container loads of software. I thought our boy was in construction."

"He is, but he obviously has a sideline in child pornography. What's the company name?"

"Triple-G Software."

"Take a look at one of those files," said Jordan. "I need an address."

After a wait of a few minutes Duignan came back to the phone. "Sorry, Ben. No sign of an address on any of these files, but I can give you the name of the trucking company that he used to move the containers."

Jordan rang the trucking company. It took him three minutes to get through to someone senior enough to help him. Steven Tobin, general manager.

Jordan identified himself and told Tobin that he was working on the Emily Carter case.

"You need to know what, exactly?" said Tobin.

"I need everything you have on this company Triple-G Software."

"I can confirm that they are a customer of ours. We ship containers for them fairly regularly."

"Where to?"

"Various addresses in Europe. Who did you say you were again?"

"Detective Inspector Ben Jordan, National Bureau of Criminal Investigation. Where do you collect these containers from?"

"I don't see the connection, Inspector, between a container and a missing schoolgirl."

"Trust me," said Jordan. "There is a connection and I need the information now. Every minute counts in our search for the girl."

"I'm sure that's true Inspector, but you must appreciate that I have no way of verifying who you are. I'm sorry, Inspector, I've already said more than I should have. You'll have to go through the proper channels."

Jordan took a deep breath. "Fine," he said. "It'll take me about an hour to get a warrant. But be advised, Mr Tobin, if the delay results in death or injury to this eleven-year-old girl I will hold you personally responsible."

After a pause, Tobin said, "Hold the line." When he came back he said, "The factory is located in a lock-up in Ringsend. Lock-up F17, behind the bus depot."

"Thanks." Jordan broke the connection.

He rang Flood. "Where are you, Liam? Have you turned up anything?"

"I'm in Clondalkin. And no, nothing."

Jordan told him about the lock-up and Flood agreed to meet him in Ringsend.

Chapter 37

Ringsend, a semi-industrial area close to Dublin's docklands, located not far from Sandymount where Kate and Lucy Jordan were living. The bus depot consists of a half-acre paved area containing several sheds the size of aircraft hangars used for cleaning and repairing the city's bus fleet. Behind the depot is a maze of narrow lanes and lock-up garages, many housing small business enterprises.

They found the group of units starting from F1 and went in search of 'Triple-G Software'. Finding no sign for the company, they counted the doors until the reached number 17. They were presented with nothing but a blank door secured with a heavy chain and padlock. Pristine snow had piled up against the door. The snowfall had stopped, but a heavy grey cloud hung overhead. Flood rang O'Reilly's number. They heard it ringing inside the lock-up. "He's in there," said Flood.

"There must be a rear entrance. Better go round the back."

Flood went off in search of a rear entrance while Jordan produced a bolt-cutter from the trunk of his car and went to work. The cutter couldn't get a grip on the padlock, but it went through the chain like cream cheese.

It was dark inside and the place smelled like a public toilet. The first thing Jordan saw was a huge pile of cardboard boxes. He tore open one of the boxes and out spilled a dozen CDs in plastic cases.

He found a light switch and flicked it on. Rows and rows of CD writers filled most of the wall space of the room.

Flood appeared in the doorway. "There's no rear entrance," he said. "If he's in here, someone must have locked him in."

Jordan handed one of the CD cases to Flood. "It's a copy shop," he said.

Flood read the label. "Triple-G Software. Office Org IV. Never heard of it."

A section at the rear was cordoned off by a curtain. As Jordan approached the smell got worse. He pulled the curtain aside.

O'Reilly's body was tied to a chair, gagged with duct tape his face and shirt covered in blood. Jordan ran his eyes over the body. O'Reilly's chin rested on his chest. His pants had been pulled down around his ankles and someone had been working on his genitals with something sharp. There was human waste mixed with blood on the floor at his feet. A thin stream of blood had run from his right ear to his collar.

Flood took one look at the body, clapped a hand over his mouth and ran for the exit. He just made it outside before losing his breakfast.

Fighting the urge to throw up, Jordan checked for a pulse, but the body was cold and rigor mortis had begun. Jordan shuddered, trying not to imagine the sequence of events. He was well used to the sight of death in all its forms, but what had been done to O'Reilly was beyond horrific. It was difficult to imagine what O'Reilly could have done to generate such anger, such sadistic cruelty. And then the snuff movie sprang to mind again. The two crimes were in the same ballpark. Perhaps they were linked.

Jordan called out the cavalry. When he'd completed the call he went outside and found Flood sitting in the snow up against the lock-up door, looking like death. His nose was running. When he saw Jordan he got to his feet, his eyes downcast like a schoolboy who'd forgotten to do his homework.

"Your first one?" said Jordan.

"Sorry." He swallowed, his Adam's apple bobbing up and down.

"No need to apologize, Liam. It's a perfectly normal reaction. It gets easier the more you see."

"Thanks for that," said Flood, blowing his nose.

Chapter 38

Jordan's phone rang.

"Jordan? Where are you?" It was Superintendent Lassiter and he was seriously pissed about something.

"I'm in Ringsend. We have a body. I'm waiting for Dr Eddings."

"A suspicious death?"

"Yes, a violent murder."

Lassiter said, "How does this relate to the Emily Carter case?"

The Super was circling like a shark in the water, looking for a weakness, an angle to attack. "The deceased is the driver of the van that was used to abduct the child."

"O'Reilly? Are you sure?"

"I'm sure he's dead, and the lab found strands of Emily's hair in his van."

"I want you back here," said Lassiter.

"As soon as I can."

"Have you seen the Daily Bulletin? They've outed Miley Richardson, His house has been attacked. A group of protesters has been throwing bricks through his windows since early morning."

Jordan said nothing. Lassiter would strike soon.

"Inspector Jordan, can you hear me? Are you still there?"

"Yes."

"We may have to relocate him. Have you any idea how much that will cost? The manpower alone could run into the thousands. And this is all down to you. Your heavy-handed approach to Richardson drew attention to him. You might as well have painted a sign on the front of his house in fluorescent paint."

Jordan felt a twinge of guilt, but no more than that. Richardson's woes were mostly of his own making, and Jordan wasn't about to take the blame for what the newspapers printed.

#

Within 20 minutes the lock-up was under the control of a Scene of Crime Unit, Dr Eddings, the State Pathologist, in attendance. He had a quick look at the corpse before speaking to Jordan. "You didn't disturb anything?"

Jordan looked at him crosswise.

"Okay," said Eddings, "but you did approach the body?"

"I looked for a pulse. When I was sure he was dead I left the scene."

"Whose mess is that in the snow at the door?"

"DI Flood of the Domestic Violence Unit. He took one look and deposited his breakfast."

"Pity," said Eddings. "Liam's a good man. I knew his father, Dominic. Another good copper. Killed himself. Tragic business."

"How did he kill himself?"

"It happened in the UK. He swam out to sea."

Jordan said, "Why have I never heard this story before now? And how come everyone else seems to know about it?"

"Everyone else?"

"Deputy Commissioner O'Malley and you."

"It was covered up. He'd left the force several years earlier. The Coroner in the UK recorded accidental death, but he'd left a note back here in Ireland. He must have been planning it for a long time." The doctor shook his head and reverted to the matter in hand. "What was your business here, anyway?"

"We were searching for Emily Carter. You do know there's a nationwide search on for a missing schoolgirl?"

"And you hoped to find her here?" Eddings fretted about his crime scenes like a bowerbird. "Never mind. Leave now, and stay away until we've finished."

Jordan left the lock-up and lit a cigarette. Two scene of crime vehicles and an ambulance stood outside. A uniformed officer stood guard at the door; a line of yellow tape had been placed across the end of the laneway where two more uniforms were holding back a gathering crowd.

There was no sign of Flood, and his car was gone. He rang Flood's number, but Flood didn't pick up. Jordan left a short message: "Where are you? Call me."

A news crew arrived. Someone thrust a microphone under Jordan's nose.

"What can you tell us about the crime scene, Inspector?" It was Declan Fairweather from the Daily Bulletin.

"Nothing," said Jordan. "The State Pathologist is inside. We will know nothing until he makes his report."

"So there is a body inside? Just one body?"

Jordan said, "I'm not authorized to speak to the press."

Somebody else shouted, "Was it a suspicious death, Inspector?"

This question was entirely spurious. Death from natural causes rarely attracted the attention of Dr Eddings and his team.

Jordan said, "No comment," and backed away beyond the microphone's range.

Chapter 39

Superintendent Lassiter rang again. "Jordan? The O'Reilly murder has been assigned to Ulick O'Shea. I expect you to give him your full co-operation."

Jordan wasn't surprised. When he'd been drafted in to the investigation, it was at the expense of Ulick. It was only a matter of time before 'the Ape' became involved again somehow.

Jordan said, "Of course."

Lassiter grunted. "I've been trying to reach Liam Flood. Where is he?"

"He's working undercover on a new line of enquiry. I expect we'll hear from him shortly."

"What new line of enquiry?"

Thinking on his feet, Jordan said, "The IRA Joint Command angle, sir. He has some shady republican contacts that might be able to get him an audience with the top men in the organisation."

Lassiter grunted again. "Well tell him to contact me asap. I've already left two messages on his phone."

Lassiter disconnected and Jordan exhaled. When his phone rang again he nearly dropped it before answering, "Liam, is that you?"

"It's Dan Payne. We've had a result, Ben."

"Quigley's on a flight to the US?"

"No, not Quigley, but we found Billy Bolger booked on a flight to Bangkok."

Budgie Bolger, O'Reilly's associate and fellow orphanage inmate.

"Is Nancy Bolger with him?"

"No, just Billy."

Jordan said, "Okay, Sergeant. Contact the airport police. Tell them to hold Bolger. I'll drive out there and pick him up. And better send a man to Bolger's house in Shankill to check on Mrs Bolger. And let Inspector Flood know what's happening."

"I thought he was with you," said the sergeant.

It was 9:40 am, nearly 19 hours after Emily's abduction.

Jordan started his car, every nerve in his body tingling with the knowledge that the case was about to crack wide open. The snow had abated, leaving a white layer four inches deep. The village roads were slippery, but passable. Keeping his speed below 50 mph he planned a route to the airport using the busiest roads as they would be clear of snow.

He'd gone a couple of miles when his phone rang again.

"Garda Irwin, here, sir. I thought I should tell you Stella Carter has left in her car. She's taken the money with her."

"Shit!" said Jordan. "I take it you've heard nothing further from the IRA Joint Command?"

"No, nothing, sir."

"What about Quigley? Has he made an appearance yet?"

"No, sir."

"Okay. I'll deal with this. Contact Sergeant Dan Payne in The Square. Ask him to send a couple of men to the airport to pick up Billy Bolger."

"Billy Bolger. Right."

"And stick by the phone. Call me if you hear anything else."

Jordan threw his car into a violent skidding U-turn. Ignoring the horns of indignant motorists on all sides, he floored the accelerator.

It was 10:10 am by the time he arrived at the drop-off point stipulated by the IRA caller, the Ashtown gate entrance to Phoenix Park. Stella's VW Golf was parked nearby. Abandoning his car, Jordan ran to the lone litter bin. He ran his eyes over the scene but failed to locate Stella Carter. A crowd of children was making the most of the unusual conditions, building snowmen and throwing snowballs at each other.

He emptied the litter bin, but found no money. Then he called Stella's phone. No answer. He moved 50 yards into the park before hitting redial, and another 50 yards before he tried again. The third time he heard a faint ring-tone coming from a thin stand of trees. He ran in among the trees and fell over Stella lying half-buried in the snow.

She was semiconscious. There was blood in her hair. Jordan lifted her head and shook her shoulders gently. He spoke her name and she opened her eyes.

"Emily. Where's Emily?"

"What happened?" said Jordan. "Did you see anybody?"

She sat up. "I put the money in the bin and hid among the trees.

Someone must have hit me from behind. Is the money gone?"

"Yes."

"Emily?"

"No sign of her. I'm sorry. I expect they'll release her somewhere else."

"You know the government refused my request to have the IRA man released. The Minister for Justice was no help at all."

This news was no surprise to Jordan.

She reached behind her head with her fingers, eyes brimming with tears. "I'm afraid we've lost her. My beautiful girl…"

Jordan helped her to her feet and wrapped his arms around her. "We will find her, Stella."

"You don't think the IRA have her at all, do you, Inspector?" She rested her head on his shoulder.

"It's difficult to be sure, but they produced no proof."

Jordan gave her a few moments as her tears flowed. Then he said, "You need to stay strong, Stella. We will find her, I promise you."

Stella wiped her eyes, blinked and looked up at him. "You really believe that?"

"I do. We have a couple of solid leads to follow. But first, we need to get you to a hospital."

Stella said, "Not necessary. I'll be fine. Go find my daughter."

Jordan called Dispatch and ordered an ambulance. He walked Stella to his car and made her comfortable on the back seat. While they waited for the ambulance he rang his old IRA contact, Packie.

"Packie, it's Ben."

"I don't have anything definite for you yet," said Packie. "I said I'd call when I have the information."

"Yeah, I know, but I really need something now."

Packie hesitated before answering. "The only lead I have is a possible meeting place, but it's no more than a vague whisper from an unreliable source."

"Let me have it."

"Mulligan's pub on the quays. But, like I say, Ben, it's nothing but a remote possibility. I need time to check it out."

"I'm out of time," said Jordan. "What about Adam O'Reilly?"

"As far as I can tell, that name is not known in any republican circles."

"Thanks, Packie."

Chapter 40

By 10:20 am, Jordan was sitting in his car, parked on the quay opposite Mulligan's bar, waiting for the landlord to open the doors. Everything was quiet.

He rang Garda Walescu.

"Have you heard from DI Flood?"

"No, sir. Where are you?"

"I'm sitting outside Mulligan's bar on the quays. I have a tip off that this is where the Joint Command hold their meetings. I'd like you to call round to the Mater hospital and check on Stella Carter."

"She's been on already, sir, looking for news. She's out of hospital and on her way home."

He terminated the call and turned his attention back to the pub. At 10:30 the landlord appeared and opened the doors. A stream of early morning Christmas shoppers passed by, most on their way to the centre of town. As the minutes dribbled by, Jordan became more and more unsettled. Packie's information was vague, unconfirmed; it could be completely wide of the mark. He could be wasting valuable time watching a building that had nothing to do with the case. He could sit there all day and see nothing. Worse, he was following the money, not the girl. Chances were the IRA Joint Command never had Emily in the first place. He should get back to The Square. Billy Bolger should be there by now, waiting to be interviewed.

As he reached for the key he saw, at the edge of his vision, a dark figure slip into the bar. Stepping from the car, he crossed the road.

It took a few moments for Jordan's eyes to adjust to the interior gloom. The pub was a shrine to everything republican, with pictures from the Troubles, the hunger strikers, bloody Sunday, and, in the centre of the mirror behind the bar, a framed copy of the Proclamation from the 1916 Rising. The landlord, too, showed signs of his republican affiliations. He wore a waistcoat over a green T-shirt, both bare arms covered in tattoos of the names of fallen IRA heroes surrounded by harps and shamrocks.

A bulky man sat at the bar wearing a brown tweed jacket and a flat cap. Jordan recognized the man's profile. It was Shane Quigley, looking for all the world like an extra from Darby O'Gill and the Little People. From the look of him Jordan could tell that the ex-NFL star hadn't slept.

"What're you doing here?" said Jordan.

Wiping his hands on a dishcloth, the landlord approached from the end of the bar.

"I'm undercover," whispered Quigley. Then, in a loud voice and an atrocious Irish accent, "Top o' the morning to you, Ben. Will ye join me in a drop of the hard stuff?"

Jordan waved the landlord away. To Quigley he said, "Where were you last night?"

"Doing my own investigation."

"Why this pub? What have you found out?"

"My sources tell me this is where the IRA Joint Command hold their meetings."

Jordan made a mental note to look into Quigley's sources later.

"And if they turn up, what're you going to do?"

"I'll think of something," said Quigley.

Jordan told Quigley how Stella had dropped the money in the park and been struck on the head.

Quigley looked up sharply. "My God! was she hurt?"

"No. She's been to a hospital and they've released her."

"But no sign of Emily?"

"Nothing yet."

Jordan walked along the bar and flashed his badge at the landlord. "Is there anyone upstairs?"

"You, me, and the Quiet Man over there are the only souls in the place."

"I'd like to check for myself."

The landlord shrugged. "Knock yourself out."

Between them, Jordan and Quigley searched the entire building, including the cellar below the bar. The whole process took five minutes. They found nothing.

Jordan brought Quigley out to the car. He lit a cigarette and offered the pack to Quigley.

"Never touch the things," said Quigley. "What's our next step, Inspector?"

Jordan looked at his watch. He needed to get back to base to interview Bolger, but if Packie's information was accurate, someone could arrive at the pub with the money soon. Could he leave Quigley to watch the place on his own?

Jordan said, "Can you stay here for a while in case our friends show up with the money?"

Quigley nodded. "You have another lead to follow up?"

"I have a suspect in custody, yes."

Quigley became agitated. "Who is he? Tell me he's the one holding Emily."

Jordan said, "I won't know until I speak to him. Park your car here. Watch out for someone carrying the sports bag. If you see it, or anything suspicious, call me, okay?"

"Ten four, Inspector."

"Promise me you won't do anything stupid."

"Scout's honour," said Quigley, raising two fingers.

"Oh, and lose the stupid cap."

Chapter 41

Jordan found DI Ulick O'Shea waiting for him in his office.

"What can I do for you, Ulick?" said Jordan.

"You can talk to me for a start," said O'Shea. "I've been waiting to interview you since 10 o'clock." He looked pained.

"Sorry about that," said Jordan. "I've been a bit busy. Am I a suspect?"

Ignoring Jordan's sarcasm, O'Shea said, "I understand you discovered O'Reilly's body. Is that correct?"

"Yes. DI Flood and I spent the morning looking for him. We finally ran him down in the lock-up at about 8:15."

"Why were you looking for him?"

"The lab identified O'Reilly's van as the one used to kidnap Emily Carter. We thought he might know where Emily is."

"And how's the search going? Have you found the child?" O'Shea returned the sarcasm.

"Not yet, but we are following a strong line of enquiry."

O'Shea leaned back in his chair. "Where's Liam Flood?"

Jordan made a production of looking at his watch. "I don't have time for this, right now, Ulick, but before you go, what can you tell me about O'Reilly's body? Has Dr Eddings turned in a P.M. yet?"

"He was tortured. You saw that." O'Shea got to his feet and strode to the door. His parting words were, "Tell Flood I need to talk to him."

"I'll let him know when I see him," said Jordan.

Sergeant Payne confirmed that a squad car had been sent to check on Mrs Bolger and she was in the full of her health. Meanwhile, the team had been busy in the Incident Room, checking phone records, not just for O'Reilly, but Bolger too, and Hughes.

"Give me the highlights," said Jordan.

"Kenny, O'Reilly and Hughes, the site foreman have been in constant contact going back several months. Two or three calls per week, minimum."

"Could be work related," said Jordan. "What about Bolger?"

"Minimal contact."

"Did you check the bank accounts?"

"We're still working through that. It's a little tricky at the weekend. We have to obtain court orders, drag senior bankers and judges from the golf course, that sort of thing." The sergeant paused. "About Dinny Kenny's bank records…"

"What about them?"

"I'm Sorry, Ben, but Superintendent Lassiter said not to go there. He said he'd talk to you about it."

Jordan rang Lassiter. "Did you put a stop on Garda Walescu accessing Dinny Kenny's financial records?"

"I did. Kenny's a wealthy man. We can't afford to go poking around his private business without a good reason."

"I have a good reason," said Jordan. "O'Reilly, one of his employees, is directly implicated in the abduction, and now O'Reilly has been murdered. Kenny is a strong suspect for both crimes."

"That's not enough," said Lassiter. "Find some evidence that links Dinny Kenny personally to either of these crimes and I'll get you a court order. In the meantime, keep out of Kenny's private accounts."

Chapter 42

The first thing Jordan noticed about Bolger was that he was no longer wearing the plaster cast on his leg. Garda Walescu switched on the tape and began the interview by recording the date and time and the names of those present. Bolger was represented by Niamh Kavanagh, one of the regular jobbing solicitors. Jordan sat across the table from Bolger and Kavanagh; Walescu remained standing.

There were spreading sweat stains under Bolger's arms and beads of sweat stood out on his forehead. The air in Interview Room 1 was as stagnant as ever, but it was not warm.

Jordan began, "Where's your crutch, Billy? And your plaster?"

"I took the plaster off," said Bolger. "I had it on long enough. The itch in my leg was driving me demented. You know how it is."

"Did you really break your leg falling through a roof?" said Jordan.

"What d'you mean? Sure I did."

Walescu said, "Your wife's a nurse, isn't she?"

Bolger glared at her. "So what?"

Walescu stared him down. "So she would know how to build a plaster for you."

Bolger blinked. "Go to hell."

"Tell me what hospital you went to," said Jordan. "And before you lie to us again, we can easily check. There are only a half dozen hospitals that you could have gone to."

"All right," said Bolger. "My leg wasn't broke. The social welfare people fall for it every time. Keeps the dole payments flowing."

"I don't believe this interview is about social welfare benefits," said the solicitor. "If it is, my client has nothing more to say. If it isn't, then please rewind the tape and start again."

Jordan nodded to Walescu. Walescu rewound the tape, and started it again.

Fixing Bolger with a stare, Jordan said, "Tell me about the snuff movies."

"What? I know nothing about snuff movies. What're you talking about?"

"We found a VHS tape in O'Reilly's house. Two young girls were abused and murdered. You were there, weren't you?"

Bolger shook his head violently. "No. O'Reilly was into all that hardcore stuff. If he had a movie like that he probably bought it somewhere."

"Like where?"

"I don't know. Holland, maybe, or Germany. You can buy sick shit like that all over Europe."

Jordan glanced at Garda Walescu. She showed no reaction. He was impressed. No doubt she'd have questions for him about his line of questioning later.

"Tell me why you killed O'Reilly," said Jordan.

Bolger's eyes opened in astonishment. "O'Reilly's dead?"

"We found him a couple of hours ago."

"I never killed him. I never killed no one."

"You and O'Reilly were close," said Jordan. "You grew up together in that orphanage."

Bolger nodded. "We were friends. Sure why would I kill him?"

"People kill their friends all the time. You killed an old friend and tried to make it out of the country. Tell me how it happened."

"It wasn't me. I swear it!" Bolger put both hands on the table, palms down. When he lifted them the table was imprinted with sweaty handprints.

"You had an argument, maybe an argument about what to do with your high profile captive. I could probably understand why you killed him, why you had to kill him. Maybe it was self-defence--"

"You have the wrong man, I swear."

Niamh Kavanagh intervened here. "My client has answered your question, Inspector. He has no knowledge of the murder of his friend. Can we move on, please."

Jordan said, "But why would you need to torture him? You must have really hated him, the way you went to work on him."

"Inspector Jordan..." said the solicitor.

Bolger was looking more and more alarmed. "I never. I couldn't torture anyone. You've got to believe me."

"Maybe you had someone else with you, someone with an even bigger grudge against O'Reilly. Who was that?"

"There was no one else--"

"You admit you killed him on your own."

"No! I never killed anyone. For God's sake, Inspector!"

Again, the solicitor intervened. "My client has denied murder and torture. If you have evidence linking him to these crimes, please produce it. Otherwise, can we move on?"

Twice more Jordan went through the interrogation, concentrating on the murder -- despite the solicitor's objections. Bolger stuck to his story: he and O'Reilly had been firm friends since childhood. He had no reason to kill his friend.

Jordan switched tack.

"All right," he said. "Let's start from the beginning. Start from when you kidnapped the girl."

"I don't know what you're talking about. I kidnapped nobody."

"We know Emily Carter was kidnapped in O'Reilly's van. You and he are close friends, and we caught you trying to leave the country. I think you were involved in the kidnapping."

"Not me, Inspector. I could never kidnap a child. If you knew--"

Niamh Kavanagh leaned forward to object, but, before she could say anything, Jordan flicked off the tape recorder and shot to his feet. "Don't give me that! We don't have time to listen to this horseshit, Bolger."

Walescu took a step forward. "Sir..."

The solicitor jumped to her feet. "Inspector!"

Bolger shook his head. "I know nothing about the girl. If you knew my history you'd understand--"

Jordan leaned across the table and lifted Bolger up by his lapels. "Emily Carter is eleven years old. We need to find her quickly, before it's too late, before she is raped -- or worse -- by your friends. Tell me where to find her."

Walescu put a hand on Jordan's arm. "Sir! Let him go, sir, please."

Jordan released Bolger, who fell back into his seat.

Niamh Kavanagh's face had turned red as a tomato. "This is police brutality," she said. "I will be making an official complaint about this, and my client will answer no more of your questions."

Walescu said, "I need to speak to you, privately, sir."

"What?" Jordan snapped. He resented Walescu's interruption. He hadn't hurt Bolger, but Ms Kavanagh had every right to complain on Bolger's behalf, and from now on, she would object to every question. Getting anything more out of Bolger would be like pulling his teeth, and would take forever.

"We need to talk, sir, outside."

Walescu held the door open and Jordan followed her outside.

Walescu said, "Let me speak to Bolger alone, sir." Jordan shook his head, but Walescu continued, "Give me five minutes with him in private."

Jordan looked at Garda Mary Walescu as if seeing her for the first time. The Garda uniform and boots made a joke of her figure, but her face was like an angel's, an angel with a secret -- radiant, assured, with shining eyes. He'd blown the interview. Surely Walescu couldn't make matters any worse than they were.

"Go ahead, Mary," he said. "I need a cigarette break."

Walescu went back into the interview room. Jordan lit a cigarette and struggled to understand what had just happened. In a desperate race against time, he had invested five precious minutes in a Garda he hardly knew, with no idea what her intentions were, or what she could do to get Bolger to talk that he hadn't tried already.

Chapter 43

As Jordan was finishing his cigarette, DI Ulick O'Shea stepped from the lift. He was sweating. "I hear you have a suspect in custody. You should have told me."

"His name's Billy Bolger. He's a known associate of O'Reilly's."

O'Shea said, "I'm aware of the connection. I'll need to interview him."

"When I've finished with him," said Jordan smoothly.

"Must I remind you that I'm investigating a particularly brutal murder?" said O'Shea.

"And I'm trying to find a missing schoolgirl. My case takes precedence."

"I'll give you an hour. After that, I'm taking over the interrogation."

"Who died and made you Commissioner?" said Jordan. "You're going to have to wait until I'm finished with him."

"You're impeding my investigation." Ulick's eyebrows began a wrestling match.

Jordan dropped his cigarette and ground it into the linoleum. "We've already had this conversation, Ulick."

"Okay, I'll wait. But I'll be watching. Leave any questions about the murder to me." He stepped into the observation room.

Jordan returned to the interview room. Bolger's eyes were downcast. He had the look of a chastised dog with its tail tucked between its legs. The capillary veins in his nose were a riot of glowing red and purple. The solicitor was white as a sheet, her eyes darting about the room like a hunted animal. Walescu looked impassive, but the colour had drained from her face. She started the tape again.

"Okay, Billy," said Jordan. "Tell us about Emily Carter's abduction."

Bolger cleared his throat. "O'Reilly grabbed her. He put her in his van." His voice shook. The solicitor made no objection.

"And what did you do to help him?"

"Nothing. O'Reilly collects all the girls."

"Girls from Eastern Europe?"

"Usually, yes. I don't know why he went for an Irish girl this time, or how he managed to chose that one."

"Tell me about the rapes, the photographs."

Still the solicitor said nothing.

"I never did any of that. They offered, but I refused. The whole thing is sick." He shuddered. "I had enough of that as a boy to last two lifetimes."

Jordan had a strange feeling of elation. Whatever Garda Walescu had said to Bolger, it had worked. Bolger was talking freely and his solicitor seemed to have lost her tongue. The case was about to crack. The elation was mixed with horror at what he was about to hear and what he would be faced with when he found Emily.

"Who abuses the children?" he said, quietly.

"Dinny and O'Reilly,"

"Dinny Kenny?"

"Yes."

"Kenny the millionaire developer? You're not spinning me a line on this?"

"Yes. Dinny Kenny, the developer."

"What about his site manager, Frank Hughes?"

"Him too."

"Anyone else?"

"There are others, but I don't know their names."

"You never do any of that stuff yourself?"

"I told you, I'm not in the club."

"Go back to the beginning," said Jordan.

Bolger took a deep breath. "You know I spent my childhood in that place. I was there from the age of eight to sixteen."

"St Benedict's orphanage?"

"Kenny was the bursar in those days. He was only in his twenties then, but he was one of the worst of them."

"You and O'Reilly were admitted on the same day."

"Yes, in 1958. They gave us the same birthday, but O'Reilly must have been older than me. He was certainly bigger than me. They gave birthdays to boys who were admitted without any papers -- you now, homeless kids. But they must have had papers for me. You see, I wasn't an orphan. I had a family, but still I was put into that place."

"Why?"

"I never found out why. I tried to for years, but I never could."

There was a serious tremor in Bolger's voice. "I expect my parents couldn't provide for me, I had a brother and a sister. I don't know. All I knew was that I had a mother and a father, a family outside." A single tear rolled down his cheek. "The staff took pleasure in reminding me, constantly. Every day I prayed that my mam would come and rescue me, take me out of that place and back to my own home." He stopped speaking. It was as if something was obstructing his airways, preventing him from getting the words out.

"But..."

"They never came. I was sure they would have if they knew what was going on, but I had no way to reach them." He sobbed.

The solicitor reached into her pocket and pulled out a packet of tissues. She took one for herself and blew her nose. She put the rest on the table in front of Bolger. Bolger wiped a sleeve across his nose, oblivious. "The people who ran that place were monsters. They used us for sex, and the beatings were merciless. We were always hungry and cold. That was down to Dinny Kenny. He looked after the money. A lot of it went into his own pocket. That was how he got started as a builder, y'know, when the place was closed down."

Jordan said, "You must have tracked down your family when you got out."

Bolger nodded. "I found them. I found them all, but they didn't want nothing to do with me. I think... I never understood why."

Bolger's tears flowed. He reached for a tissue and blew his nose. Jordan gave him 15 seconds to collect himself. Walescu fetched him a glass of water.

Jordan said, "What about O'Reilly -- was he abused?"

"At first he was, but then he became a 'handler'."

The solicitor said, "A handler?" Her voice had developed a tremor, too.

Bolger continued, "Handlers were older boys who helped the staff. They taught the younger boys what to do, fetched them from their beds at night, dished out punishments and rewards, and sometimes they joined in."

Jordan said, "Joined in? In the abuse, you mean?"

"Yes, and the beatings. We hated them. We hated them even more than the staff."

"So you hated O'Reilly. Is that why you killed him?"

Bolger stared straight into Jordan's eyes. "Yes, I hated him, and I'd love to be able to say I cut off his balls and killed him, but it wasn't me."

"Go on," said Jordan, making a mental note to return to this later.

"When the place was closed down, Kenny gave jobs to a lot of the boys -- the handlers, mostly. They set up a paedophile ring. Additional members were recruited and it grew."

Jordan said, "I thought it was rare for abused kids to become abusers."

Bolger shook his head. "Don't you believe it, Inspector. Abuse invades the mind, and incubates there. It's a contagion, a cycle that never dies." He glanced at Walescu. "A cycle that must be broken."

"Who else was at the orphanage when you were there?"

"I knew about fifty boys who were around about my age. I don't remember many names, but I remember all the staff and I remember every one of the handlers."

"Was Hughes at the orphanage when you were there?"

"No. I don't think he was ever in there. He joined the club when he started working on the building sites for Kenny."

Jordan gave Bolger a few more moments to compose himself. Then he said, "Why were you leaving the country?"

"That girl, Emily Carter. I knew how much trouble she was going to cause for Dinny and the others. I wanted to get away from that."

"So you knew about Emily. You were involved."

"I knew, but I wasn't involved."

"You're totally innocent. Is that what you're saying?"

Bolger shook his head again. "I used to bring the girls food."

The solicitor placed a warning hand on Bolger's arm, but said nothing.

Jordan said, "So you are a member of this 'club'. How long was this going on?"

"The club started about a year after the orphanage was closed. 1985."

"But you never abused any of the kids."

"Never. I saw that they were fed."

"Why didn't you go to the Guards?"

Bolger suppressed a sob. "I couldn't. Kenny would have had me killed. He used to say 'every chain has a weakest link' and I didn't want to be the weakest link in his chain."

"You're a miserable excuse for a man, Billy. You know that, don't you?"

Finally, the solicitor, spoke again. "There's no call for insults, Inspector."

"I think you killed O'Reilly. You killed him because you hated him. And I think that's why you were running away."

"No, I've told you. That had nothing to do with me."

The solicitor said, "My client has repeatedly denied any involvement in the murder of O'Reilly, Inspector."

Jordan stopped the tape and wound it back. "Listen to this," he said.

The tape replayed Bolger's words, "Yes, I hated him, and I'd love to be able to say I cut off his balls and killed him, but it wasn't me."

"I told you only that we'd found O'Reilly's body and that he'd been tortured. I never said anything about his balls."

Chapter 44

Bolger shuddered. "I saw his body, but I never laid a finger on him. I swear. I went to the lock up. I wanted to tell him how stupid he was picking up the daughter of two celebrities. I wanted to rub his nose in it."

"And you found his body. You never touched him?"

"It was horrible. I've never seen anything like that before. And now I can't get it out of my mind. I reckon O'Reilly's having the last laugh."

"Was the place locked when you got there?"

"No, it was open. I locked it when I left."

Jordan sat back. "Okay, so who do you think killed O'Reilly?"

"I don't know, Inspector. I can think of lots of people who might have wanted him dead."

"People who would torture him first?"

Bolger broke eye contact and muttered, "He made a lot of enemies."

"In the orphanage, you mean?"

"There and later on. He wasn't an easy man to like."

Jordan changed the subject. "Where does Kenny get the children from?"

"Eastern Europe, mostly. Bulgaria, Albania, Romania."

"Supplied by whom?"

"Various suppliers. I'm not sure."

"Peter Green? Was he one of the suppliers?"

Bolger nodded.

Jordan thought: Flood will be happy to hear this news. He'd finally have something concrete the throw at that piece of blubber, and something to justify the beating he dished out to him. He glanced at Walescu, and he could see from her expression that the same thought had crossed her mind.

"Tell me how Kenny operates," said Jordan.

"He has a lot of projects on the go. A big payroll means big cash flow problems. The money from sales of his properties comes in big, infrequent chunks. Meanwhile, he has to keep injecting cash into his business day by day to pay his labour force."

"The banks?"

"Yeah, I'm sure he has several bank overdrafts, but it's never enough, so he makes ready cash from the girls. He buys them in, photographs them and sells them on. The pictures make him a lot of money."

"Who buys the girls? Where do they go?"

"It varies. There's a Turk who takes a lot of them, but Dinny'll sell to the highest bidder."

Keeping his voice level, Jordan tried the big one. "Okay, tell me where they keep the children, Billy."

"Kenny has several houses. He moves the kids around."

"Houses that he owns?"

Bolger swallowed a mouthful of water. "One he owns, the rest are rented."

Walescu handed a pen and pad to Bolger. Jordan said, "Write down the addresses."

Bolger wrote down three addresses in slow, childlike handwriting. When he was finished Walescu went off to arrange the search warrants. Jordan glanced at the clock. It was 12:30 pm, 21 hours and 30 minutes since the abduction.

Jordan met O'Shea at the door to the interview room. O'Shea's hands were fists like hairy dogs at his sides. "I thought we agreed you wouldn't ask any questions about O'Reilly's murder."

Jordan shrugged. "As long as he was getting it all off his chest, I thought we might get a confession out of him."

"We agreed. Didn't we agree that?"

"You suggested it, Ulick, I never agreed. I have to ask any questions that might help us find Emily Carter."

O'Shea smouldered for a few moments. "As of now, I'm taking over this interrogation."

Jordan shook his head. "Bolger's given us a couple of locations where we might find Emily. You can have him after we've checked them out."

Chapter 45

Dinny Kenny clutched a phone to his ear. "I'm sorry, Yuri. She's not on the ferry. I know I let you down."

The Russian spoke at the end of the phone line, "I am very disappointed. You agreed to send her across today."

"I know. She escaped. My men didn't lock her up securely."

"You promised to me. I promised to my customer, and I'm sure he promised to his customer. Just like the Pony Express or the stagecoaches in Siberia, one dead horse and the whole chain is breaking down."

"I will deliver her by four o'clock tomorrow."

"You have her?"

"I will have her soon. My men are out looking for her now."

"You mean you hope. You don't have her. You hope you will find her. You hope to deliver her to me tomorrow."

"I'm confident, Yuri, trust me." After a couple of beats, the developer said, "We could deliver this afternoon. There's a later ferry my man could catch."

"What time?"

"The ferry sails at four. We should get to you by seven."

"That could work. I might still have time to pass her on to my customer."

"That's settled, then," said Kenny.

"And the price? You will take something off the price?"

"Of course," said Kenny, grimacing. "We can take a thousand off the price."

"Five t'ousand, I think."

"Five thousand."

"Seven o'clock. Disappoint me again and there will be more than a dead horse to worry about. Do I make myself clear?"

"I won't let you down again, Yuri."

"I hope not," The Russian said. "The last man who disappointed me was found in pieces in the Volga--"

"It won't be a problem--"

"--the Don--"

"No worries, you'll get the girl--"

"--and the Vistula."

Chapter 46

Jordan and Walescu drove out to the first address on Bolger's list, a house in a redbrick terrace on the North Circular Road. Walescu took the wheel. The roads were like ice-rinks caked with tightly-packed snow.

"What was that about snuff movies?" said Walescu.

Jordan glanced at her. Her posture looked a little rigid, but her face showed no great stress.

"I found a tape cassette under the floorboards in O'Reilly's house. It was... pretty horrific stuff."

"Probably foreign as Bolger suggested," she said, her voice tight.

The house was locked, bolted and boarded up, front and back. Jordan used a crowbar to prise a front window open. They searched the house, top to bottom. The place was empty, and there were no signs of recent habitation.

The second house on the list was in Brabazon Street in the inner city. This house looked lived in, but nobody answered when they rang the doorbell. Jordan gave the ornate door knocker a workout, but the door remained firmly closed. The application of his boot close to the lock persuaded the front door to let them in, and both Walescu and Jordan conducted a quick search of the building. The place was devoid of furniture, the floorboards in every room bare.

Garda Walescu called to Jordan from an upstairs room. "Come and look at this, sir."

When Jordan joined her she pointed to a metal hoop set in the wall.

Fingers of ice ran down Jordan's back. The hoop was exactly like the ones he'd seen at the orphanage. He peered out through a window at the snow-covered city. It was a week before Christmas. Bright sunshine and the crisp air made the scene looked positively Dickensian. About two miles away as the crow flies across the roofs, the top two floors of Harcourt Square were visible.

Walescu ran a palm across her forehead. Jordan could see she was distraught. He said, "Don't worry about it, Mary, we'll find her soon."

"I thought this was it," she said. "I really thought we'd find her here."

The third address on Bolger's list was St Benedict's orphanage. Back in the car Walescu said, "That's it. We searched the orphanage yesterday." She yawned.

Jordan said, "I'm not keeping you awake, I hope, Garda.

"Sorry, sir. Rough night."

Chapter 47

Emily opened her eyes. She didn't know how long she'd been asleep, but thought it must be the middle of the day -- her tummy was making hungry noises. She slid off the bed and tried the door. It was locked. She put her ear to the door and listened. She could hear the murmur of conversation. Several times the conversation died and Emily thought the farmer might have gone to the neighbours, but each time the murmur started up again.

Then she heard a phone, an old-fashioned ring-ring, very loud. She banged on the door. The woman opened it.

"What is it, dear?" she said.

"I heard a phone."

"Yes, dear. The phone people must have repaired it. Come on, you can call your parents. She took Emily into the hall where the farmer was talking on the phone. It was an old black instrument with a circular dial and a braided cable connecting the handset to the receiver. The farmer finished his call and handed the phone to Emily. It was heavy.

Emily rang home. Her mother picked up straight away.

"Mammy, I'm safe," she said. "I escaped! Please send Daddy to take me home."

"Oh Emily, darling, are you all right?" There was a sob in her mother's voice.

"I'm fine, Mammy. Tell Daddy to come and get me."

"Where are you, sweetie?" Her mother's voice broke.

"I'm not sure." Emily turned to the farmer, "Where am I?"

He took the phone. "Emily is safe with us," he said. "We'll call back in a few minutes," and he replaced the phone on the receiver.

"But I didn't tell Daddy where I am. He doesn't know where to find me." Emily felt her lip tremble.

"That's okay, a cushla," said the woman. "We'll call back in a little while and let him know where you are."

Emily said she was hungry and the woman cooked her a meal of fried eggs and bacon with soda bread and salty butter. It was delicious and Emily gobbled it all up in silence. After the meal, the woman took Emily back into the bedroom and closed the door. Emily heard the key turn in the lock. She looked out the window. The sun was shining. The snow had stopped, but the landscape was blurry white. Even the trees were barely recognizable. She tried the window. It slid open, providing her a means of escape. But her coat, her shoes and her socks were still by the fire. She could manage without the coat, but she couldn't manage without shoes. She searched the room and found a pair of wellington boots in a wardrobe. They were too big but she put them on and climbed out the window.

Wading through the snow, she rounded the farmhouse and descended the hill to the road. Without looking back, she set off down the road. She walked and slithered for a mile or so, and then at last she heard a car coming from behind her. She thought it might be her father, but it wasn't his. Her daddy's car was a blue Lexus. This was a big car, but it was black and it wasn't a Lexus. It approached and slithered to a halt beside her.

The man inside wound the window down. He wore a black coat with a curly fur collar and black leather gloves. He said, "Where are you off to, young lady? You look like you could use a lift."

"No thank you," said Emily. She walked on and the car followed, its wheels making a strange crunching sound in the snow, like paper crumpling.

"It's very cold," said the man. He seemed friendly, but she was wary of him. "I'd never forgive myself if I left you here with no coat, to freeze to death. Where are you off to?"

"Home," said Emily.

"And where's home?" he said. He had a funny nose that crinkled as he smiled.

"Stepaside," said Emily.

"Well, there's a coincidence," said the man, beaming at her. "That's just where I'm going. Hop in and I'll give you a lift."

Chapter 48

Jordan rang Dr Eddings, the State Pathologist, and asked for an update on O'Reilly's post mortem.

"Ulick O'Shea's on that case. Talk to him," said Eddings.

"I need to hear it from the horse's mouth."

Eddings laughed. "Not over the phone, Ben."

"Put the kettle on, Doc. I'll be there in fifteen minutes."

Jordan dropped Garda Walescu off at The Square and drove to the morgue in Marino.

He found Dr Eddings in his office drinking tea from his famous mug, inscribed 'Who's a Big Boy Then?'

Eddings said, "Someone really hated our friend. You saw what they did to his hands, his genitals, his eyes."

"His hands?"

Eddings nodded. "They broke most of his fingers."

"What about the damage to his eyes? Was that before or after...?" Jordan threw the doctor an enquiring look.

"Ante-mortem, I'm afraid."

"Any idea why?" Jordan spoke through clenched teeth.

"Your guess is as good as mine, Ben. The broken fingers suggest that he was tortured for information, but the gag is difficult to explain if they were expecting him to speak. The rest is just plain nasty. Whoever did this bore the victim one hell of a grudge."

"What about the time of death?"

"That's a little tricky, given the cold temperatures, but I'd say about four to five hours before you found him. Say between three and four in the morning."

"Would he have made a lot of noise?"

The doctor scratched his ear. "I'm sure the poor guy screamed his head off, but the gag would have stifled most of it. It's unlikely there was anyone in any of the other lock-ups at that hour, but even if there had been they probably would have heard nothing."

"And the cause of death?"

"The shock from the genital mutilation would have killed him, likewise the injuries to his eyes, but my vote goes to the brain injury.

A deep puncture wound caused by a thin implement inserted through the right aural cavity."

Jordan shuddered. "A stiletto in his ear? That's positively medieval!"

"Something like that, yes, only not tapered. Maybe a skewer or a sharpened screwdriver."

"A gimlet, maybe?"

"Not long enough."

Before leaving the morgue, Jordan rang the Technical Bureau and asked to speak to Eddie Duignan.

"We don't have a lot to tell you," said the senior technician. "The CDs in the lock-up were all loaded with child porn -- pretty hardcore -- all identical copies. It was obviously a manufacturing operation. We found no traces of Emily in O'Reilly's home or the lock-up where he was killed. And in the lock-up itself, by the way, we found very little trace evidence of any kind: no hairs or fingerprints, not much more than a flake of skin that wasn't the victim's. Whoever killed him was extremely careful."

Jordan said, "Was this the work of more than one person?"

"Impossible to tell."

Jordan disconnected and his phone rang immediately.

Superintendent Lassiter said, "Where are you? Is Flood with you?"

"I'm at the morgue and no, sir. I haven't seen Flood for a while."

"Damn his eyes," said the Superintendent. "I need you to go to the Carter house right away. Emily has contacted her parents."

Relief swept over Jordan like a tsunami. "She's safe? Where is she? What did she say?"

"Get out there and find out." The super hung up.

Jordan put his siren on and pointed the car at the southern foothills of the Dublin Mountains.

A great calm descended on him as he drove. Emily would soon be reunited with her parents. Once that happened, his career as a garda inspector would come to an end. The prospect of re-inventing himself and starting afresh filled him with hope, but he had given little thought to what he might do. He could certainly get work as a manager or an advisor for the security industry. Or how about 'Ben Jordan, PI'? He quite liked the sound of that. His music would provide other options. He could see himself sitting at the piano keys in a smoke-filled bar somewhere exotic, like Casablanca.

O'Reilly's death was a puzzle that remained to be resolved, but Jordan would happily leave that to Ulick O'Shea to sort out.

Chapter 49

The scene at the Carter-Quigley house in Stepaside was like a military base preparing for an imminent attack. Garda officers prowled about speaking in low tones while others sat glued to their telephone monitoring equipment.

Shane Quigley was there playing the part of officer-in-charge. Jordan asked Garda Irwin, the phone monitor, for an update on Emily's phone call.

Quigley said, "Stella took first the call. Emily said she was safe, but she didn't say where she was. Then another voice, a man's voice, took the phone and said he'd call back in a few minutes."

"And did he call back?"

"Yes. He said he was looking after Emily and he would see that she came to no harm, but he wanted a finder's fee."

"A finder's fee. How much?"

"He didn't say. He rang off. We've been waiting for him to call again."

"When was this?"

Quigley looked at his watch. "The last call was at one thirty. I'm not sure when the first one came in."

Garda Irwin said, "The first call was at 1:22, sir. It lasted one minute twenty seconds. The second call was at 1:28 and lasted less than a minute."

"No hope of a trace, I suppose?" said Jordan.

"Sorry, sir." Irwin looked miserable.

Quigley said, "The men are all primed, and I have a direct line to Rory O'Malley. As soon as we get a location the operation can start."

Jordan put on a pair of headphones and listened to recordings of both calls. Emily's voice sent goose bumps leapfrogging up and down his spine. She sounded weary, but healthy. The man was elderly, with a strong country accent. He sounded hesitant, almost apologetic. It was clear what must have happened. Emily had escaped from her abductor and stumbled into this man's world. He was planning to capitalize on his good fortune.

Jordan removed the headphones and said to Quigley, "When he does call back and demands a ransom, a finder's fee, whatever he calls it, you must agree to pay."

Quigley opened his mouth but, before he could object, Stella Carter stepped into the room and said, "We will pay. I don't care how much he asks, we will pay."

"I thought you said the money you gave to the IRA Joint Command was all you could raise," said Jordan.

"It was," said Stella.

Looking like the cat that got the canary, Quigley produced the sports bag from under a table. "I recovered the cash from the terrorists."

Jordan did what he could to hide his surprise. "I hope you didn't hurt anybody."

Quigley laughed. "Piece of cake. The guy came into the pub alone and unarmed. A slippery dude called Dwyer. He used to work for Stella. I took the cash from him."

"Just like that?"

"Well, no, he put up a bit of struggle, and he threatened to kill Emily. Inspector Flood hit him a couple times and he admitted that the IRA didn't have her. They never had her." He beamed.

"DI Flood was there?" said Jordan.

"Yeah, I reckon he was tailing the IRA man."

It was good to know Flood was still on the case, even if he had assumed the role of Scarlet Pimpernel.

"Okay," said Jordan. "You must agree to pay this finder's fee. With careful planning we should be able to recover Emily without actually paying out anything."

Stella turned a steely eye on Jordan. "We will pay the ransom," she said. "I want no interference from the police. I won't allow any tricks. My daughter is too precious for that. Whatever this man asks I will give him in return for my daughter."

"Understood," said Jordan, "but you will need our help to ensure that the exchange goes without a hitch. We have a lot of experience of this sort of thing--"

Stella put her hands together as if in prayer. "You're not listening to me, Inspector. I want no police involvement of any kind. We can't afford to risk spooking this man. Shane will handle the exchange. Alone. And that's my final word."

As Jordan slipped his coat on in the hall, Garda Irwin touched him on the elbow. "We did have one other strange call, sir," he said.

Jordan put the headphones on again and listened to the recorded call.

"Tell Stella Carter that the White Knight is on her daughter's case. Believe me when I say that whatever ordeal is visited on the child will be repaid a thousand-fold. But whoso shall offend one of these little ones which believe in me, it were better for him that a millstone were hanged about his neck, and that he were drowned in the depth of the sea."

It was the voice of DI Liam Flood.

Chapter 50

Jordan returned to Harcourt Square. Once he got out of the country and into the suburbs he made good time as the relentless Christmas traffic had cleared a lot of the snow from the roads.

Flood's office was empty. Jordan tried his phone once more, and when he got no answer, he began a search of Flood's desk. He found nothing to explain the young DI's absence until he tried to open the top drawer on the right. It was locked.

Garda Walescu came into the office and said, "Sir? What are you looking for? Maybe I can help."

"Do you know where Liam is?" he said.

"No, sir. I haven't seen him since he left to meet you at Ringsend."

"Do you have a key for this drawer?"

Frowning, Walescu said, "I don't think Inspector Flood would be happy for you looking at his private stuff, sir."

"Get me something to open it. A nail file, a screwdriver, anything. We need to find him. He hasn't been seen for six hours."

Walescu left and returned with a knitting needle. "Will this do?"

Jordan used the needle to spring open the desk drawer and went through the contents. He found a King James Bible, an unlabelled VHS cassette and a black and white photograph of a group of children and adults lined up outside a massive redbrick building. Jordan recognized St Benedict's Orphanage. The concrete fascia bearing the words: 'The Home For Lost Children' was clearly visible.

Walescu looked closely at the picture. She pointed to a tall boy in the second row. "This must be Liam's father."

There was no mistaking the tall, good-looking youth. Jordan said, "I didn't know Liam's father was at St Benedict's."

"Oh yes, sir, didn't he say?"

"No, he didn't." Jordan pointed to one of the adults in the back row. "There's Kenny. Do we know anyone else in the picture?"

Walescu shook her head. She picked up the video cassette. "We should check this out."

Jordan took it from her. "Leave that with me."

Walescu picked up the Bible and rifled through it. "It's been highlighted, and Liam has made lots of notes in the margins."

"Do we have any explanation for that?" said Jordan.

Walescu closed the book and replaced it in the drawer. "This was his father's Bible. I think it meant a lot to him, growing up in... that place. It was all that he had to hold on to as a child, and it was the most precious possession that he left behind for his son."

Jordan took the VHS cassette to his own office. He locked the door before placing it in his cassette player and pressing 'play'. Within seconds, the skin on his scalp was crawling again. He ejected the cassette angrily, threw it into a desk drawer and locked it. It was a duplicate copy of the snuff movie.

Chapter 51

Jordan took the lift to the cells. Bolger's cell was empty. O'Shea.

He ran to the ground floor and burst in to Interview Room 1. Bolger was sitting at the table with the solicitor, Niamh Kavanagh, beside him. Across the table sat O'Shea and one of his officers. Jordan could tell that the interview had barely started.

O'Shea shot to his feet. "Get out of here, Jordan!"

Jordan held up a hand in a placatory gesture. "I just need Billy's help with something."

"You're interfering with a murder inquiry. Get out, now!"

"Just a couple of minutes, Ulick, and then I swear I'll leave." He placed the photograph on the table in front of Bolger.

"What is this?" said Bolger's solicitor. "This is most irregular."

"It's all right, Niamh," said Jordan. "I just need Billy to take a look at an old photograph."

The solicitor nodded to Bolger and Bolger peered at the picture, angling it to catch the overhead light while eliminating reflected glare. "That's me there," he said, pointing. "I was skinny as a pikestaff in those days. This is the head. We called him Nosy because of his nasal hair. His real name was Nostrus." He pointed out some more people in the picture. "There's Kenny at the back, grinning. This boy behind me is Flood. This one over here is Adam O'Reilly."

"Was Flood a handler?" said Jordan.

"Not while I was there." A shudder ran through his body and he pointed to one of the adults, tall and thin, standing at the back beside Kenny. "This character here is Farsteel. He was the worst of them."

"Where is he now?"

"He died in '92. That bastard was a total sadist. Should have been locked up. He used to take boys to the dungeon and beat them senseless, but not before..." He swallowed.

The solicitor said, "I think you've said enough."

Jordan's heart rate accelerated suddenly. "Where was this dungeon?"

"My client will answer no more questions until you explain this line of questioning, Inspector."

Bolger ignored his solicitor. "That was what we called the cellar where most of the really vicious stuff happened."

"Where was the entrance to this cellar?"

"A trapdoor under the stairs."

Jordan took the lift back to the sixth floor and burst into Superintendent Lassiter's office. The superintendent was buried in some document.

Jordan said, "I need a search warrant for St Benedict's Orphanage."

Lassiter looked up, squinting, as if he suffered from snow-blindness from all the white paper he had to read. "You've searched that building already. You said it was empty."

"I have new information that may lead us to Emily Carter."

Lassiter said, "Very well, call Tierney. Take an Armed Response Unit with you."

"No," said Jordan. "I'd rather handle this on my own."

"Why do you have to dispute every detail with me? Tierney's men are highly trained. You have nothing to worry about."

"With due respect, the last thing we need is lots of guns at the scene. I'd hate to spook Emily's captors and start a gun battle. All I need is a dog handler."

Lassiter waved a dismissive hand and returned to his document.

It was 3 pm, 24 hours since Emily's abduction.

Jordan parked at the gate of the orphanage to wait for the dog handler, but after five minutes he stepped out of the car. Light, soft rain was falling now, turning the snow to slush, the shrinking snow drifts clinging on in sheltered areas, under trees and up against walls.

Jordan took his 'enforcer' from the car. Then he opened Walescu's door and said, "Go around the back and create a diversion while I get in through the front."

"Shouldn't we wait for the dog handler?" said Walescu.

"Probably," said Jordan, "but every minute could be vital."

Garda Walescu circled the property, wading through wet slush to the high wall at the back. Once there, she began to shout. "Here, dogs, come and find me." She whistled and shouted some more.

As soon as the three dogs set off around the building, Jordan climbed over the gate and ran to the front door. The heavy metal enforcer bounced off the door on his first attempt. On his second, the door sprang open. Jordan stepped inside and, as the dogs came hurtling around the corner of the building toward him, used the enforcer to jam the door shut behind him.

To the sounds of the dogs barking and hurling themselves against the front door, Jordan hurried to the door under the stairs. He opened it and located the trapdoor. But before he could open the trapdoor he heard a noise from a room somewhere above him. He went to investigate.

As he climbed the stairs he heard voices that gradually became more distinct. He recognized Kenny's voice first, reasoning, pleading. The second voice was more difficult to identify, as it was screaming obscenities. Jordan advanced toward the sounds.

He came to an open door. Inside the room he could see Kenny, dressed in a full-length coat with an astrakhan collar, spread-eagled against a wall.

The second voice was shouting, "You destroyed him. You and those other butchers destroyed a generation of young men. I'll give you a minute to say a prayer. That's more than you ever gave my father."

Jordan recognized the voice.

Chapter 52

Jordan stepped into the room. DI Flood was pointing a handgun at the developer's head. Flood's gun hand was shaking, and there were tears streaming down his face.

Jordan said, "Give me the gun, Liam."

Flood looked up, his eyes ablaze. "Stay out of this, Ben. This is a private matter between me and Dinny. Mr Kenny is about to pay for his past misdeeds and the sins of the rats that ran this stinking hole."

"Calm down, Liam," said Jordan. "And put the gun down."

"I'm going to finish this here and now. He's a putrid pile of shit."

Kenny turned his eyes toward Jordan. "Please don't let him shoot me."

"Remember your oath, man," said Jordan. He took a step forward. "Give me the gun."

"Stay back, Ben, I'm warning you."

"He's not worth it, Liam. D'you really want to spend the rest of your life behind bars?" The snuff movie leapt into Jordan's consciousness. He wondered what he would do right then if he was the one holding that gun. He was pretty sure he would have no qualms about pulling the trigger. Kenny was guilty of countless crimes against children, and he was implicated in the movie. He certainly facilitated it, even if he hadn't been one of the participants.

"He killed O'Reilly." Kenny whispered. "He tortured him. He told me."

"I made him talk. He was a worse rat than this one. My father told me what he did to him and the other boys. Can you imagine what it must have been like in this place? My father was six years old when he first came here. The abuse started on his second day -- his second day! He turned to an older boy for help. Unfortunately, he chose Adam O'Reilly. And that choice killed him. It took years, but O'Reilly was just as responsible for my father's death as if he'd cut his throat. An eye for an eye..."

Jordan held a hand out toward Flood. "Put the gun down, Liam. We need Kenny. He's the only one who knows where Emily is."

Flood ignored him. "I've waited years for this moment. This monster and his friends destroyed my father, deprived him of his childhood, beat him, starved him, and submitted him to persistent and unrelenting sexual abuse -- from the age of six."

Jordan said, "You had some justification for what you did to O'Reilly, Liam, but if you kill a second time... Do you really want to throw your life away?"

Kenny turned to face Flood. "For God's sake, listen to him."

Flood carried on with his litany of complaints. "Life in this place left scars on my father, and not just physical scars, although there were plenty of those. The emotional scars went much deeper. Imagine the torment he went through every waking moment and every night in his nightmares. To end it, he drowned himself. He was only 42 when he died. It's a miracle that he married and had a son. It's a miracle that I was born at all.

"What my father needed from the age of six was care and affection, and what did he get? Hatred, starvation, brutality and unimaginable depravity. The children in this place were treated like objects of no more value than animals or pieces of furniture--"

Flood stopped to brush a sleeve across his eyes and Jordan took a step toward him. Flood was distracted for a moment, and Kenny pounced. Moving with surprising speed, he grabbed Flood's wrist, forcing the gun upward. It went off with a crash, bringing down a chunk of plaster from the ceiling. Jordan took two more steps forward, but before he could intervene, the gun swung down between the two men and went off a second time.

Chapter 53

Flood's knees buckled, and he slid to the floor.

Jordan put his head down and charged. The developer fired again. Jordan felt the bullet whistle past, the percussion deafening him in one ear. He caught Kenny in the midriff in a rugby tackle and Kenny fell backwards, the gun flying from his hand with a clatter.

They wrestled on the floor. It was an uneven contest. Jordan had the advantage of his Garda training and his Judo black belt, and Kenny was 20 years his senior.

Disentangling himself from Kenny, Jordan stood over the developer, lying on his back on the floor. But Kenny had pulled a handgun from a coat pocket and it was pointed at Jordan's chest.

The gun was tiny, but it could still be lethal and Kenny couldn't miss from that range. Jordan raised his palms. "Hold your fire, Kenny," he said. "I can testify that you shot Flood in self defence, but kill me and you'll go down for murder. I'm unarmed."

"Back off," said Kenny. Jordan did so, and Kenny got to his feet.

"Tell me where the girl is," said Jordan. He glanced at Flood. He was bleeding heavily from a stomach wound, but his groans told Jordan that he was still breathing.

"Turn around," said Kenny, waving his gun.

"Get help for Flood and we can still salvage the situation," said Jordan as he turned his back to Kenny.

The developer delivered a single glancing blow with the gun to the back of Jordan's head. Jordan fell to his knees. Then he lost consciousness.

When he came to, Jordan took a moment to recover his senses. Then he phoned Dispatch and gave them the address. "I need an ambulance. An officer has been shot. And tell that dog handler to get here fast."

He hurried to the window. No more than a few seconds had passed. Kenny was past the dogs in the garden and facing Garda Walescu who stood in his path outside the front gate. Walescu held up a palm and ordered Kenny to stop.

Kenny pulled the small gun from his pocket and fired. Walescu fell, and Kenny ran for his car.

"Oh shit!" said Jordan. He turned away and said into his phone, "I now have two officers down with gunshot wounds."

Then Jordan heard another shot, much louder than Kenny's peashooter, louder even than Flood's Garda regulation SIG P226. He looked out the window. Kenny was on the ground. Emily's father stood over him, a heavy, smoking revolver in his hand.

Jordan checked Flood's condition. The DI was on his back, breathing heavily, clutching his stomach and staring upwards as if obsessed by the light fixture in the ceiling. Blood was pumping from his wound, a pool of it spreading across the floorboards.

Jordan ran down the stairs and opened the front door. Three sets of snarling teeth greeted him. He slammed the door and jammed it shut. The dogs flung themselves at it. Then he returned to attend to Flood, closing and locking the bedroom door.

He removed his jacket to make a pillow for Flood. As he lifted Flood's head, Flood reached up and grabbed Jordan's forearm with a bloody hand. "Ben, is that you?"

"Take it easy, Liam. Help is on its way."

"I can't see you. Did Kenny get away?"

"I'm right here, Liam" Jordan said. "Kenny's been shot. He's going nowhere."

"I didn't kill O'Reilly, Ben. I hurt him, his fingers, but I never did those other things to him." Flood was racked by a terrible cough. "He was alive--"

The front door crashed open, and Jordan heard the dogs bounding up the stairs. Then they were barking hysterically and throwing themselves at the bedroom door. The door shook, but the lock held. Moments later Jordan heard the dog handler climb the stairs, and a couple of minutes after that the handler had the dogs under control.

Jordan unlocked the bedroom door and returned to Flood's side. The blood flow had eased. Pale as death, Flood had lost consciousness.

An ambulance drew up. The paramedics jumped out and began working on Garda Walescu. A second ambulance arrived almost immediately and Jordan called to them. The second paramedic crew dashed up the stairs to attend to Flood, but it was too late. Flood's battle was over.

Still feeling the effects of the blow to his head, Jordan stumbled down the stairs and outside to where Garda Walescu lay on a gurney. Walescu was conscious, wounded high on her chest, close to her shoulder.

"How are you, Mary?" said Jordan.

"I'm okay," she said. "Have you seen Liam? I heard two shots."

"The medics are with him," he said.

Garda Walescu was rushed to hospital in the first ambulance. The second team of paramedics placed Dinny Kenny on a gurney and went to work on him.

Jordan approached a dazed Shane Quigley, his hand hanging by his side, holding a massive Smith & Wesson revolver, still smoking. Jordan took the gun. "Why did you shoot Kenny? He knows where Emily is."

"I realise that now," said Quigley. "When he shot that female officer, I reacted without thinking."

The way he said 'that female officer' sounded false. Jordan said, "Her name's Mary Walescu."

"Mary Walescu. Right," said Quigley, and Jordan knew then that she was Quigley's information source.

Jordan looked at Kenny lying on the gurney, a red stain spreading on his chest. "How is he?" he asked a paramedic. "I need to talk to him."

The paramedic stood back, shaking his head. Kenny's sardonic smile was still there, a little lopsided now.

"Tell me where you've put Emily," said Jordan.

"You know you're dying," said Jordan. "Do one good thing in your miserable life and tell me where you've hidden Emily Carter."

"She's already been shipped out of the country. You'll never find her. You're too late."

"Where have you sent her?"

"Go to hell." Blood trickled from Kenny's mouth.

Quigley leaned his weight in over Jordan's back. "Tell us where she is, you pervert," he snarled.

Kenny's mouth filled with blood. He gurgled and the light in his eyes died.

"Stand back," Quigley shouted. "I'll shake the information outta him."

Jordan put a restraining hand on the American's chest. "It's no good, Quigley. He's dead."

Chapter 54

Jordan felt as if his head was about to split open. He went back into the building, to the sound of the second ambulance siren drawing away. He lifted the trapdoor and called, "Emily?" down into the dark. There was no answer. He went down a few steps. Quigley clicked a light switch above him and followed Jordan down. The single bulb did little to illuminate the area, but there was a bed and a couple of studio lights lying scattered on the floor. Jordan looked under the bed and checked behind the steps. There was no sign of Emily.

Quigley gasped. "My God. Is this where they held her? These are arc lights. The bed... Here's a camera."

Jordan recognized the scene of the snuff movie in which the little Romanian girl had been beaten to death. There was no mistaking the bed and the miserable little Christmas tree in the corner. Once again scenes from the video forced themselves into Jordan's mind. Gritting his teeth, he said, "We've no proof that Emily was ever here."

But after a few moments, Quigley exclaimed and emerged from behind the stairs holding a schoolbag. He thrust the bag into Jordan's hands.

"You're sure this is Emily's?"

Quigley showed him Emily's stickers and marker slogans. "She was here." He touched the child's handwriting, tears bursting from his eyes. "We're too late."

Jordan suppressed a strong urge to throw up. "We may find her still. She could be out there somewhere. Let's see if we can work out where she went."

They hurried outside. The three dogs were tied to their restraining bar looking sullen.

"How the hell did she get past the dogs?" said Jordan.

"She.... She could make dogs do anything for her." Quigley was already speaking of his daughter in the past tense.

"We'll have to ask her how she did it when we find her," said Jordan. He looked at his watch. It was 16:20, over 25 hours since Emily's abduction.

Chapter 55

Jordan did a quick survey of the property, trying to put himself in Emily's shoes. There was no way of guessing which way she could have gone, and darkness was falling. Jordan knew that whatever chance he had of tracking Emily in daylight, it would be impossible in the dark.

Quigley staggered near to the dogs, and they reached out their noses, whining eagerly, and sniffed Emily's schoolbag.

Jordan whirled and spoke to the dog handler. "Come with me, and bring one of the dogs with you."

The dog took Emily's scent from her satchel, circled the building, gave a yelp, tugged on the lead and set off into the wood, towing the handler. Jordan followed, and Quigley followed Jordan, hugging the schoolbag to his chest.

Within minutes they were in almost complete darkness. The dog followed a path flanked on both sides by densely planted trees. The handler gave the dog its head and they had to run to keep up. The path narrowed, then disappeared altogether. The dog pitched into the trees and the handler pulled it back.

"We can't follow it in there," he said. "We have two options. I can let it off the lead and we can find our own path through the wood and hope to meet up with the dog again..."

"Or?" said Quigley.

"Or, we can keep it on the lead, find a better way forward and hope that it picks up the scent again."

"Not much of a choice," said Jordan. "Either way we'd be depending on luck."

"But if I release the dog and it finds Emily it might attack her," said the handler.

That settled it. They hunted for a less tangled path and went forward that way. The dog was miserable, and kept trying to move off into the undergrowth to its right. Jordan took that as a good sign. It was still picking up the scent.

After ten minutes they emerged from the wood onto a country

road. The dog surged left and followed the road, then plunged up a hill towards a farmhouse.

Quigley beamed as Jordan banged on the door. An old woman answered the door, an elderly sheepdog by her side. The two dogs immediately began barking, hackles raised. It was all the handler could do to hold on to the guard dog's lead.

The old woman closed the door in their faces and the three men waited. The guard dog continued to bark, straining at its leash. When the woman opened the door again the sheepdog had vanished. They could hear it barking from somewhere inside the house.

Jordan flashed his badge. "We're looking for Emily Carter," he said. "The dog followed her scent here."

"She was here early, but she left." The woman stared innocently at them.

"What time was this?" said Jordan.

Quigley said, "What d'you mean, she left?"

The woman looked alarmed at Quigley's bulk and his aggressive manner. "She arrived at about seven. The poor little mite was tired and wet through. We put her to bed, but she climbed out through a window."

"When was this?" said Jordan.

"I suppose she left at about one o'clock."

"Where did she go?" said Quigley.

"I'm sorry, I don't know. Just a minute." The woman went inside and returned with a pair of shoes and an overcoat. "She left these behind her."

Quigley reached in and grabbed Emily's shoes and coat.

"Are you saying she left the farmhouse through a window wearing no shoes?" said Jordan.

The woman bit at a nail. "She stole a pair of my son's wellingtons."

"Emily rang home from here?" said Jordan.

"She did. We gave her shelter, the poor thing. We would have returned her to her parents if she'd stayed with us."

Quigley stepped forward. "You demanded money to give her back. You said you'd call back. Why didn't you?" One of his hands had become a fist. With the other he clutched Emily's belongings to his chest.

"She -- Emily -- left us. There didn't seem much point in ringing back again."

Quigley's face was turning puce. "You could have told us where you were. We could have tracked her from here, she could be safe by now. Anything could have happened to her after she left here."

"God, I'm sorry," said the woman.

"Let me in," said Jordan. To Quigley, he said, "You wait here. I won't be long."

The woman showed Jordan the room where she'd put Emily.

Jordan checked the window. He said, "You should never have let her wander off in the snow."

"We never wanted that to happen," said the woman.

"You were trying to negotiate a ransom."

"Not a ransom, just a finder's fee, a little reward. That would have been fair."

Jordan watched her coldly. "I hope for your sake we find her safe and well. If not, I'll be back and you may be charged with obstruction, kidnapping maybe."

"But we were trying to help," she whined.

Chapter 56

Jordan and Quigley left the farmhouse and returned to the road. The dog tugged at its leash, leading the handler along the road to the right, down a slight incline. Three minutes later the dog stopped and began searching in circles, its nose close to the ground. It covered the area three times before sinking to the ground with a whimper.

"He's lost the trail," said the dog handler. "She was probably picked up by a car."

Jordan looked around him. To the left of the road the ground fell away into a broad valley with a village visible between the trees. To the right, the Dublin Mountains bathed in a light white blanket, still. If Emily had been picked up by a friendly motorist, she would have made it home by now. She must have been recaptured by one of Kenny's men. They would have been searching for her. What had Kenny said? "You're too late. She's gone."

Jordan rang The Square and requested a car. While he waited he reviewed what he knew. Kenny had a well-oiled route for shipping children out of the country once he'd finished with them in his photographic studio. O'Reilly used containers to ship out the child pornography, disguised as office software.

"I think I know where she might be," said Jordan. He rang Dipar Transport and asked to speak to Steven Tobin, general manager.

"When was the last time you picked up a container for Triple-G Software?"

"Yesterday, Inspector. We delivered a 20-foot container to Dublin port for shipment to the UK, final destination Rotterdam."

"Containing what?"

"17,500 software CDs."

Jordan disconnected and rang Victor Massey, an officer he knew in the Customs & Excise office at Dublin port. He asked Massey to check whether the container had shipped.

"It should have shipped today at noon, but the sailing was cancelled due to bad weather," Massey told him. "It's on board the vessel and the vessel's still here. It's due to sail in the next 60 minutes."

"Take it off the ship, Victor, and hold it until I get there."

"I'm sorry, but that's impossible," said Massey. "The container is on a truck somewhere on the car deck. We can't remove one truck without unloading the whole ship."

"Why can't you unload the ship?"

Massey snorted. "That would take hours. The ship would miss the tide and we'd have to pay the shipping company for loss of earnings. It would cost a fortune. We call that the 'nuclear option'. But if you get here before the ship sails, you can go aboard, find the truck and search the container, even if you have to sail with it."

"Right. Why don't you start without me," said Jordan.

"What are we looking for?"

"An eleven-year-old girl."

Chapter 57

The Square came up trumps, ordering a car from the nearest Garda station, at Kilternan. Jordan got in beside the driver. Quigley, the dog handler and the guard dog took the back seat. The dog put its head on Quigley's lap. "Can't we leave the dog?" he said plaintively.

"We may need him," Jordan said. Then, to the driver, "Get a move on, son. We have a ferry to catch."

They made it to Dublin port in 15 minutes. Victor Massey, the Customs & Excise man, was waiting for him on the pedestrian gangway.

"We've checked that container, Ben. There's nothing in it but cardboard boxes full of CD's."

"Are you sure?" said Jordan. "Maybe you missed her. She could be sedated."

Victor Massey said, "My men know what they're doing, Ben. If there was anything living in there they would have found it. Trust me."

"She's got to be in there," said Jordan, wearily. "I don't know where else she could be. How much time do we have?"

Massey checked his watch. "She must sail within the next twenty minutes."

"If we can't find the girl we may have to hold the ship," said Jordan. Massey led the way up the gangway onto the ship. The dog handler followed with the dog, and Quigley followed them.

Massey said, "You could try, Ben, but the captain is king here. He's not going to cancel a sailing without convincing evidence that the girl's hidden on board. Do you have any?"

Jordan shook his head. "Not really. It's just a strong suspicion."

Jordan directed the dog handler to the passenger area. Quigley followed the dog handler.

It took the dog four of the 20 minutes to pick up Emily's scent.

"Over here!" shouted the handler as the dog chased a figure down a passageway. Jordan recognized the body-shape before he saw the face. It was Frank Hughes, the building site manager, moving like an Olympic sprinter.

They lost him and emerged on the car deck. Jordan and Quigley cast around, then the dog gave a high, baying bark and dragged the handler forward. They found Hughes crouched beside an SUV, holding Emily in his grip. She looked groggy.

Hughes had one arm across Emily's chest. He held a knife at her neck.

"Stay back," said Hughes above the noise of the turbines and the barking dog. "Come any closer and I'll slit her throat."

Quigley yelled, "Emily!" and Emily replied, "Daddy!"

"Take it easy, Hughes," said Jordan. "What's your plan?"

"The ship will sail in a few minutes. When we dock on the other side I can disappear."

"Give her to me and I'll let you go," said Jordan.

"I don't think so. I'm holding the child until I'm free and clear."

"You don't think the British police will be waiting for you whatever I do?" said Jordan.

"If they are, the child will die," said Hughes.

"Let her go, you bastard!" Quigley roared.

"Daddy!"

"I'll let her go when we dock on the other side. You just have to make sure I get there in one piece."

Jordan looked at Emily. She seemed alert, now. He said, "All right, Hughes. We'll get off the boat and tell the captain he can sail."

"You can't leave her with that maniac," Quigley hissed to Jordan.

Jordan said, "We don't have a choice, Quigley. We need to get off the ship."

Jordan, Quigley and the dog handler turned toward the door.

With a flurry, Emily broke free from Hughes's grasp. Hughes grabbed her at the neck by her coat. Emily twisted around to face him and kicked him on the shin. "Daddy, save me!" Thin as a mosquito's wing, her voice echoed off the bulkheads.

In one movement Jordan turned back, drawing Quigley's revolver. The dog handler unhooked the dog's collar. Silent as a ghost, the German shepherd rocketed forward, leapt at Hughes, and fastened its jaws on his forearm. Hughes and the dog went down together like a sack of turnips.

Emily ran to her father, and Quigley scooped her up in his arms.

The handler dragged the dog off Hughes. Jordan put him in cuffs.

Within five minutes they had left the ship, it had slipped its mooring and was carving a channel out of the port toward the Irish Sea.

When Massey got off his walkie-talkie, he grinned and said to Jordan, "Thanks for the collar, Ben. I've alerted the lads over in Liverpool."

"Tell them to check the contents of those CDs while they're at it," said Jordan.

Chapter 58

Back at The Square, Jordan took a call from the lab.

"About that snuff movie," said Eddie Duignan. Instantly, Ben stiffened. "It was made in 1986, as far as we can reckon. It's from one of DI Flood's open cases. He sent us a copy two years ago. Flood has identified the children. They were sisters from Romania. The girl that survived is called Marja--"

"They weren't both killed?"

"No. The younger of the two survived. Didn't you watch it all the way through?"

"No. Did you?"

"Sure, Ben. It's my job."

"And how did it make you feel?"

Duignan hesitated before answering, "It made me sick, Ben, how d'you think it made me feel? But we have to remain objective."

Jordan marvelled at the technician's off-hand attitude. Surely this was taking scientific objectivity to extremes. He said, "Have there been other movies like this?"

"No. This was a once-off, as far as we can tell."

Jordan did a little mental arithmetic. If the younger child in the movie had been nine or ten when it was made, that would make her 27 or 28 years old now.

Deputy Commissioner O'Malley beamed, "I wanted to congratulate you on a job well done, Ben. It reflects well on the force. There's nothing like a happy picture for good publicity, and Emily's smiling face makes the perfect happy picture."

"Thank you, sir."

"I was deeply shocked to lose Liam Flood. He was an outstanding young detective."

Jordan looked at his hands. "He'll be missed."

"He will. Now, tell me about Mary Walescu."

"Garda Walescu is as able an officer as I've met..." said Jordan.

"But?"

"I think she needs to be reassigned. The Domestic Violence Unit is a bit rough for such a young officer."

"Liam Flood selected her," said O'Malley.

"Yes, sir, she told me. Even so, I think she's been in there long enough. She could use a change of scene."

Jordan placed the envelope containing his letter of resignation -- now a little dog-eared -- on the DC's desk. O'Malley made no move to pick it up. Steepling his hands, he put his fingertips to his lips and said, "You know how much I value your work, how much I trust you. I'd hate to lose you." Jordan tried to interrupt, but, leaning forward in his chair, O'Malley continued, "I'm bumping you up to Acting Superintendent and putting you in charge of ODU until further notice. Superintendent Lassiter has been suspended pending an Internal Affairs enquiry into his involvement with Dinny Kenny, and I've asked Briscoe to take over his brief."

Jordan shook his head. "Thank you, sir, but I've given it a lot of thought. I don't think I'm cut out for police work any more."

"It's ODU, isn't it? Give me a day or two. Let me see if I can find you a more active role. Superintendent Murphy will be retiring next year. I can't make any promises, mind, but you should be a shoo-in there."

Murphy ran the Special Detective Unit, one of the most active units on the force.

"No, sir, it goes a lot deeper than that. For every low-life that we put behind bars, there seem to be two waiting to take his place. It feels like all I'm doing is moving piles of shit around. It's destroying me and my marriage."

DC O'Malley sighed. "This is a mistake, Ben. You'll lose the best part of your pension. What on Earth will you do with yourself?"

Chapter 59

Jordan bought a copy of the Daily Bulletin and a bunch of grapes on his way to the hospital. The headline story in the newspaper took his breath away. It was about a man who hanged himself in his home in Tallaght. A convicted paedophile, hounded and terrorized by the public beyond endurance, his name was Miley Richardson.

Garda Walescu was well on the mend, free of medical monitors, sitting up in bed, knitting.

Jordan placed the grapes and the newspaper on the bedside locker.

"How is Emily?" said Walescu.

"She's well. I'm not sure she realises how lucky she was. What are you knitting?"

She held it up to show him. "It's a jacket for my niece in Bucharest. Do you like it?"

"Lovely," Jordan said. "Hughes is singing his brains out."

Walescu paused to pop a grape into her mouth before resuming her knitting. "He's done a deal with the DPP?"

"I expect so. Interpol are rounding up paedophiles and child traffickers all over Europe. But he'll still do a long stretch -- Bolger too."

"What about Green? I think he is the main trafficker of children from Eastern Europe."

Jordan nodded. "He's out of the country, but he'll be picked up when he returns."

"Excellent!" She offered Jordan a grape. He took one.

"I wanted to ask you why you volunteered for the DV unit," he said. "Domestic Violence and Sexual Abuse is hardly an ideal posting for a young Garda."

"A young female Garda, you mean." She smiled.

"You had a personal interest in this case, didn't you?"

"Did I?"

"When did you first enter the country?"

"I told you, I studied English. I came here when I left school at nineteen."

Jordan said, "You were here before that, though, weren't you?"

"Was I?"

"I think you were here much earlier. I think you were abducted and brought to Ireland as a child."

She laughed and popped a grape into her mouth.

Jordan said, "Tell me what you said to Billy Bolger. How did you get him to talk?"

Walescu turned her attention back to her knitting. "I told him a story."

Jordan waited, and Walescu began, "The story is about two sisters Marja and Leticia, living on a farm in Romania. They had two older brothers. At the start of the story Marja was nine, Leticia was eleven. They were happy living on their farm. They went to school, they helped their father and their brothers to care for the animals. Happy, happy, happy. The sun always shining. On Sundays, they went to church. The pastor told the people about good and evil, about how God's justice brings everything into balance in the end. Some days, evil may win, but sooner or later, good triumphs and the balance is restored. Leticia and Marja understood nothing of this, really. They knew nothing of evil.

"Then one day, some men came and stole Marja and Leticia away. The girls were brought to Ireland where they were put in chains. Here they found out the meaning of evil. Until then, they had no idea that such men existed." She laughed. "The younger sister, Marja, didn't even know that Ireland existed. She was just nine."

"You were abused. How did you escape?"

"The two sisters were taken to a dark place where two men used them for sex. Then, one day, the men began to beat Leticia. Marja watched as they beat and beat and beat her until she was dead. Marja's life ended on that day too. She swore she'd find a way to balance God's justice, even if it took the whole of her life."

"She must have been terrified that the same thing would happen to her."

"Oh, she was. She lost the power of speech for two years. She was sold to some other men in England. She listened to the men speaking and she began to learn English. After a couple of years in England she was taken to the Middle East. That part of the story was bad, but not as bad as the night she watched her sister die. Then she escaped. It took her eight years, but she made it home to Romania. Her mother was dead, her father had lost the farm and his mind."

After a long pause Walescu said, "She was seventeen. She studied

English more, and when she was ready, she travelled back to Ireland to put things right."

Jordan said, quietly, "And she got her revenge."

Walescu turned her head towards him. Her eyes brimming with tears, she said, "No, not revenge. To help put a stop to it, to save other children from what happened to her, and to break the cycle."

"Last night," said Jordan, "remember when the lab rang with the news that they'd found a hair from Emily in O'Reilly's van? You sent out all those APBs."

"Yes, I remember."

"I went out to O'Reilly's house and met Liam Flood there. I got back to The Square at 3 o'clock. If anyone asks, we met there then and worked through the night on the case."

She smiled, swapped the needles over, and started on the next row.

Chapter 60

Emily was given a clean bill of health at Crumlin's Children's Hospital and sent home. A childcare worker asked her later in interview if the men had done anything to her, she replied, "They gave me an injection that made me sleep."

"Anything else?" asked the childcare worker.

"Yes, it was horrible. They smashed my phone."

Reunited with her bike and her glasses, her overt distress was soon swallowed up by the excitement of Christmas.

Jordan called out to the house.

Stella Carter offered him a drink and he accepted a glass of lemonade. He was off duty.

"How's Emily?" he said.

"She has a slight head-cold, and she's a little clingy, but she's going to be fine. The doctors say she will soon recover and become the confident, happy child she was. I can't thank you enough for saving her. We owe you everything."

Emily ran into the room, out of breath and laughing. "Mammy, have you seen Daddy? He's hiding on me."

"No, dear. He hasn't been through here. I'd like you to meet Mr Jordan, Emily. Say hello."

"Hi." And she ran out of the room again.

Jordan laughed. "And how are you and Shane?"

"I'm well, thank you, and Shane too. You know we're planning a big wedding in the New Year?" She laughed. "I wanted something quick and cheap, but he's insisting on a big splash. He says he needs all the publicity he can get."

Shane Quigley made an appearance as Jordan was leaving, and Jordan asked him where he got the information about Mulligan's pub and who alerted him to come to the orphanage. Quigley refused to answer these questions, citing 'the Fifth Amendment'.

#

Emily was given her own security detail; a man accompanied her everywhere she went, and for a few weeks she became a celebrity at school. She told all her friends how her daddy rescued her. Her best friend Aimee made her retell the whole story from the beginning, over and over. They completed their Darfur project together.

The bond between Emily and her father grew stronger after her ordeal, and Stella began to make more time from her busy schedule for her daughter. Emily quickly discovered that she had not just one but two loving parents.

Her surprise Christmas present that year was a Labrador puppy. She discovered that housetraining a puppy was more difficult than controlling fully-grown guard dogs.

O'Shea interviewed Quigley about his shooting of Kenny and possession of an illegal firearm. Jordan looked in on the interview. The American made a lot of indignant references to 'the Second Amendment'. Jordan reckoned a file would be sent to the Director of Public Prosecutions, but no action would be taken against Quigley. His gun would be confiscated.

Ulick O'Shea stepped into Jordan's office as he was emptying the contents of his desk into a cardboard box.

"I heard you were leaving," said O'Shea.

"Afraid so, Ulick. You're going to have to manage without me."

"I need a moment of your time before you go, old man."

Jordan picked up the box. "Sorry, old man, I'm not a member of the force anymore."

"It won't take a minute." Jordan put the box down again, and O'Shea continued, "I've read your report on the Carter case. You claim that Liam Flood killed O'Reilly."

"That's right. He confessed to me."

"He could have been lying."

"You doubt a deathbed confession?"

"Yeah, but I have a couple of other suspects for the crime."

"Like who?"

"Billy Bolger for one. The lab boys have found skin traces from Bolger at the lock-up."

"Doesn't prove a thing. He admits he was there and saw the body and, as I said, Liam Flood confessed to the murder."

"O'Shea scratched at his wrist. The hair on his arm was growing like a creeper around his watchstrap. "Garda Walescu's a strong suspect, too, Ben. The lab reckoned more than one person could have been involved, and the absence of trace evidence suggests another garda."

Jordan shook his head. "I don't think so. Garda Walescu has an unbreakable alibi."

"Oh?"

"She was here with me that night."

"Doing what?"

"Working on the case."

"All night?" O'Shea's eyebrows did a quick Riverdance routine.

"Try sleeping while an eleven-year-old schoolgirl is missing."

O'Shea tucked his hands under his armpits. "You'll have to explain Flood's motivation and exactly what happened."

"Of course. I'll write the report for you if you like."

"Just give me the facts," said O'Shea. "I'll write my own report."

Chapter 61

Christmas Eve. Ben rang the doorbell of his old home in Sandymount and waited for his wife to answer the door. He felt ridiculous ringing his own doorbell, but he couldn't walk in uninvited. He stood with his back to the door looking across Dublin Bay. The tide was in, but turning, the murky water scarred with white wavelets all the way to the hill of Howth. Under heavy grey clouds rolling in from the north, the hill looked like a malformed cake covered in a light sprinkling of icing sugar. Between the clouds and the sea, lone gulls circled and called to one another of the threat of fresh snow and a hard winter ahead.

Kate opened the door. A flicker of surprise, then she stood aside to let him in. He handed her a bottle of wine decorated with a red ribbon.

Lucy was sitting by the fire in the front room. "Daddy!" She threw her arms around his neck as if she hadn't known that he was coming. The gesture was artificial and too unlike Lucy to fool anybody, least of all Kate, but it was just what the situation demanded. Ben had no opening line, nothing he could say that wouldn't open Kate's wounds, and he knew Kate had none either. Lucy was their only hope.

He and Lucy exchanged presents. Kate found glasses and opened the wine. And then they were all together, sitting around the fire like a normal family, Kate and Lucy sipping their wine, Ben nursing a tomato juice. Lucy rattled on, skipping from subject to subject. She seemed unwilling to leave the two of them alone; it was clear she didn't trust them to discuss their differences without another major falling-out. And then Lucy ran dry. She yawned, stretched her limbs and went off to bed.

It was time for Ben to take the lead, to make the first move, but before he could say anything, Kate said, "It's never going to work, Ben." He tried to say something, but she held up a hand. "No, don't interrupt me. I've given it a lot of thought. I'm not blaming you. I know it's not your fault. You have a high pressure job, so do I. Our marriage would never have worked. I see that now. My parents were right about that, although for all the wrong reasons."

"You've found someone else, is that it?"

She gave him that wide-eyed look that could have meant anything from surprise to guilt. "Don't be crazy, Ben."

"So who was the man who answered your phone on Saturday last?"

"Saturday? That would have been Dave. He was home from London for a sales meeting. He called round to see how I was."

Her brother.

"Lucy--"

"Lucy's old enough to accept the situation for what it is. She's an adult. I'm sure she understands. And we owe it to her not to carry on living a lie. It's time to move on, time for both of us to start afresh."

"So what you're saying is our marriage won't work as long as I'm with the police."

"That's about it, Ben."

"What if I told you I'm leaving the Guards?"

She gave a short derisory laugh. "You? Leave the force? It's your whole life."

He said quietly, "I've already resigned. I handed in my resignation two weeks ago."

"Hah! And was it accepted."

"Not immediately. Rory O'Malley tried to get me to change my mind. He offered me a promotion. I turned him down. I only stayed on to help find Emily Carter."

She ran her eyes over his face. "You really mean it?"

"Uh-huh. I'm no longer a copper, effective immediately."

"Don't you have to work a couple of weeks' notice?"

"No. That wouldn't work in the Guards. They can hardly put me on some new case. I've cleared my desk."

"But why Ben? I hope you didn't resign on my account."

"Not entirely. The job was starting to get me down. I need to get out while I'm still young enough to try something else."

She pressed him some more on his reasons. It took some time, but he managed to convince her that the grinding, oppressive nature of the work had finally got through to him. He had simply grown weary of it all.

"What will you do?" She said. "I can't see you pottering about the garden or keeping pigeons."

Ben smiled. "I haven't given it much thought. I expect I'll think of something."

Later, he went into the back room, opened his piano and began to play. He played his mother's favourite song, Take My Breath Away.

Then he played for Kate.

In the morning it was snowing again. He couldn't remember the last white Christmas in Dublin.

THE END